She couldn't stop the visions of death.

She didn't *want* to see that. She wanted to see what everyone else saw, an ordinary painting of a vase of flowers. She wanted that more than anything.

But when she glanced back at the still life one more time, she knew with painful certainty that what she was looking at was someone tumbling helplessly down a steep flight of stairs, screaming in terror.

Terrifying thrillers by Diane Hoh:

Funhouse
The Accident
The Invitation
The Train
The Fever

Nightmare Hall: The Silent Scream
Nightmare Hall: The Roommate
Nightmare Hall: Deadly Attraction
Nightmare Hall: The Wish
Nightmare Hall: The Scream Team
Nightmare Hall: Guilty
Nightmare Hall: Pretty Please
Nightmare Hall: The Experiment
Nightmare Hall: The Night Walker
Nightmare Hall: Sorority Sister
Nightmare Hall: Last Date
Nightmare Hall: The Whisperer
Nightmare Hall: Monster
Nightmare Hall: The Initiation
Nightmare Hall: Truth or Die
Nightmare Hall: Book of Horrors
Nightmare Hall: Last Breath
Nightmare Hall: Win, Lose or Die
Nightmare Hall: The Coffin
Nightmare Hall: Deadly Visions

NIGHTMARE HALL

Deadly Visions

DIANE HOH

SCHOLASTIC INC.
New York Toronto London Auckland Sydney

No part of this publication may be reproduced in whole or in part, or stored in a retrieval system, or transmitted in any form or by any means, electronic, mechanical, photocopying, recording, or otherwise, without written permission of the publisher. For information regarding permission, write to Scholastic Inc., 555 Broadway, New York, NY 10012.

ISBN 0-590-20298-7

12 11 10 9 8 7 6 5 4 3 2 1   5 6 7 8 9/9 0/0

Printed in the U.S.A.   01

First Scholastic printing, February 1995

Deadly Visions

Prologue

I can't believe she saw it. The last person I would have expected.

There they were, all of them, gathered around the painting, not one of them suspecting there was anything unusual about it.

And then here she comes, this little nothing who knows squat about art, and announces the truth.

I could have strangled her, right then and there, with my bare hands. Probably should have. Wish I had.

No, that's not true. Right there in public, in the middle of a crowd? Losing my cool would have ruined everything.

Well, if I don't stop her, she's going to do exactly that. Ruin everything.

No problem. Of course I'll stop her. That insignificant little ignoramus isn't going to spoil all my fun.

I'll see her dead first. The little twit won't live to see another Monday.

How shall I do it?

Something clever, something truly . . . artistic.

Chapter 1

In the crowd of close to seventy-five people milling about in the lobby of Salem University's Fine Arts building, viewing the newest exhibit of paintings, sketches, sculptures, jewelry, and other works of art, only Rachel Seaver thought she saw a figure drowning in one of the paintings.

Her friends scoffed when Rachel tried to point this out to them.

"I don't see anything but a seascape," her roommate, Bibi Jensen, said flatly. "Not a very good one, either, if you ask me. It looks kind of like something my six-year-old sister Tessie would bring home from first grade."

"I concur," Joseph Milano, who had two of his own paintings on display, said with mild disgust. "The artist probably hung the canvas on a wall, stood back, and took aim, tossing handfuls of blue and green paint until the tubes were empty."

Ignoring him, Rachel continued to study the seascape. It was untitled, with no identifying card tacked beneath it. And there was no signature on the painting.

Aidan McKay, another Fine Arts major and the real reason Rachel was at the exhibit, smiled and said, "I didn't believe you when you said you didn't know much about art, Rachel. Now, I think maybe you were telling the truth."

As the three moved away to study other artworks, Rachel stayed where she was. Her eyes never left the large, unframed canvas. Alive with vivid blues and brilliant greens, it hung on an end wall of the spacious lobby, and it seemed to Rachel that most of the spectators were passing it by, spending far more time on the surrounding paintings.

She didn't see why. The seascape was beautiful, so rich with color, alive with the tumult of storm-tossed waters. The sky in the painting was an ominous slate-gray, contrasting sharply with the vivid colors.

"That's all wrong," a short, stocky boy with dark, curly hair, wearing a white shirt and a white apron said as he passed Rachel. He lingered for a moment, a large, round tray full of glasses in his hands. "The sea is never that color during a storm. It's always the same color as the sky, a heavy, dark gray, topped off by whitecaps. The artist doesn't know what he's doing."

"I thought," Rachel said tartly, "that painters were supposed to interpret things as they see them, not as everyone else sees them."

The waiter laughed rudely. The expression on his face as he shrugged and moved away into the crowd said yeah, right.

"Who is that guy?" Rachel asked, annoyed, as Bibi returned, clear plastic cup in hand.

"Rudy Samms," Bibi answered with a wide grin. "Isn't he gorgeous?"

"Yeah, if you like the Neanderthal type. Interesting that his name should be Rudy, as in Rude-y. Atrocious manners."

"Well, keep your hands off him," Bibi warned. "You're here because of Aidan, remember? You leave Rudy the Rude to me." She left again, calling over her shoulder, "And don't wait up, okay?"

Rachel sighed. Bibi had no more interest in art than she did in astronomy. Rachel had talked her into attending this exhibit by reminding Bibi that there would be males present. Bibi had recently broken up with her boyfriend, Paul, nicknamed Apollo because he looked like a Greek god. In Rachel's opinion, he also had the brains of a thimble. She had hoped that this time Bibi would find a guy who knew what an intelligent thought was and could articulate it, but here she was setting her sights on Rudy.

Not, Rachel thought, someone I would want to double-date with if Aidan McKay ever asks me out.

Bibi was tall, blonde, and gorgeous, and probably could have dated any guy on campus. Leave it to her to zero in on the most unpleasant person in the entire lobby. Bibi was a great roommate, but she had far better taste in clothes than she did in men.

Rachel studied the painting again. She was absolutely convinced that amid the turquoise and kelly green and azure blue she saw a figure struggling in the storm-tossed waves. She could understand why no one else saw it. The arms were no more than blobs, flailing wildly above the water, the head an elongated dab of pinkish-colored paint, the eyes dark daubs, the mouth a slash of red.

But the eyes were wild with fear, the mouth, if that was what it was, open in a scream of terror.

The image chilled her spine, as if someone had slipped ice cubes down her back.

Why was she seeing something no one else could see?

Aidan and Joseph were both art majors. If there was a figure valiantly struggling against the waves in the painting, wouldn't they see it?

They hadn't. Nor had Bibi.

Rachel moved forward and peered more intently at the painting. Viewed that closely, all of the colors blended together in a green and blue haze. She stepped back again, frowning and running a hand through her short, dark, curly hair, something she did constantly when she was frustrated or confused. "I may not know anything about art," she muttered, "but I know what I see, and what I see is someone drowning."

"No, you don't," Aidan said, coming up behind her, putting his hands on her shoulders. Leaning forward, he spoke into her ear. "That is a seascape, Rachel Seaver, and not a very good one, frankly. That's all it is. The question is," he added, moving around to stand beside her, "why would you *want* to think you see someone drowning in that painting? Are you always that morbid?"

Looking up at him, ready to respond as heatedly as she had to the waiter, Rachel thought again how nice-looking Aidan McKay was. Not gorgeous like Apollo-the-dimwit or Rudy-the-rude, but *nice* looking, with a lean, angled face and sharp blue eyes. Her eyes were blue, too, but hers were a quiet blue, like the sky in midwinter, while his were the brilliant blue of a blazing July sky. His hair was brown with a hint of red. It was as wavy as hers, and he wore it long. She had to clench her fists to keep from reaching out and touching it.

Chill, Rachel, she warned herself. You just met him the day before yesterday, and you hardly know him.

"It's not that I *want* to see someone drowning," she said, less defiantly than she'd spoken to Rudy Samms, "it's just that I *see* it. I can't help that, can I?"

Aidan looked at the painting again. "No, I guess not," he said. He shrugged broad shoulders in a white T-shirt. "To each his own. But you have some imagination, kiddo."

She wasn't terribly happy with the "kiddo," and she felt a pang of resentment at being told that her imagination was leading her astray. But the fact was, she really *didn't* know anything about art, and he did, so until she could find out who the seascape artist was and maybe confirm what she was seeing, it seemed silly to keep arguing about it.

Still, she couldn't help it if her heart went

out to the agonized figure drowning in the stormy sea.

She glanced at the painting one more time, looking for a signature.

There wasn't any. Not even initials.

"You don't know who painted this, do you?" she asked Aidan as they moved together toward the corner where Joseph and Bibi were standing.

"Nope. The truth is, we were all so busy getting ready for this exhibit that we didn't pay much attention to what anyone else was working on. I don't remember seeing any seascapes, though."

"Maybe Joseph will know."

Joseph didn't. He and Bibi were talking to a tall, thin girl with frizzy dark hair that fell to her waist. She had on a huge, floppy straw hat with fat red roses wound around the brim. More roses were clustered at the neckline of her long, black chiffon dress, which Rachel suspected had come from an antique shop. The girl had a strong, square face and huge, dark eyes, heavily made-up with jet-black eyeliner.

Why doesn't she just hang a sign around her neck that reads *Aspiring Artist*, Rachel thought, amused. Talk about dressing the part.

"This is Paloma Lang," Joseph said, nodding toward the tall girl. "Designs jewelry. Her real name is Jane, but she says no one would buy jewelry from someone named Jane, so she changed it."

"I think," Rachel said gently, "that there is a jewelry designer named Paloma, isn't there? Paloma Picasso?"

"Exactly," the tall girl said with a shrug. "I mean, it worked for her, right? Of course, I intend to be twice as successful as she is."

"Then maybe you should have changed your name to Paloma Paloma," Joseph joked.

The subject of his joke gave him a barely tolerant smile. "Very amusing." Then to Rachel, she said, "Want to see my jewelry? It's getting a lot of attention. No surprise there. People never expect to see anything but paintings at these exhibits. They're always thrilled to see something different. Especially when it's good."

Rachel found Paloma's lack of humility startling, but refreshing. It was more than self-confidence, and yet didn't seem arrogant. Paloma simply knew that she was good at what she did. Rachel wondered if the artist who had painted the seascape had the same easy pride in his or her work.

As Paloma led her away, Rachel glanced over her shoulder toward the seascape, thinking the artist might be lingering near it somewhere, anxious to see what kind of reception it got. But there was no one at all near the painting. People were passing it by without much more than a casual glance.

So maybe it was a good thing the artist wasn't there, she thought. Weren't most artists terribly sensitive about their work being ignored?

Except, of course, someone like Paloma. Ignoring Paloma Lang, who talked loudly and gestured theatrically with her jeweled fingers, would be almost impossible. And that probably went for her work, too.

Which was, Rachel realized when she saw the pieces neatly displayed in a glass case, very good. The surprisingly delicate and amazingly intricate necklaces, bracelets, and earrings were truly beautiful.

"You *are* good," Rachel said in awe, studying the jewelry carefully.

"Of course I am," Paloma agreed, nodding. "I've been doing this since I was eight. I made a necklace out of a vine and some acorns at summer camp. When the other girls saw me wearing it, they all wanted one. So I made more and sold them. I went home from camp with twenty dollars more than when I got there. My parents were thrilled." She flicked a long, slender finger toward one piece in particular, that of a three-strand gold chain adorned with tiny gold acorns. "That first necklace looked something like this. Don't you love it?" She smiled confidently as they turned away from the display case. "I expect to be very, very rich one day." And then added bluntly, "Do you?"

Rachel laughed. "Do I expect to be rich? I don't know. Hadn't thought about it. I haven't even decided what I want to major in." She was torn between teaching and a career as a journalist. Both appealed to her.

"Well, you'd better plan to be rich," Paloma said, "so you can afford to buy my creations. Because they won't come cheap." Then, in that same blunt way, she asked without warning, "Speaking of designs, I saw the way you smiled at Aidan. Do you have designs on *him*?"

Rachel felt her face flushing. She shrugged in an effort to appear casual. "He seems nice. Why? Do you?"

"Me?" Paloma looked astonished. "Date a fellow artist? Do you think I'm mad? Artists are all hypersensitive, egocentric, and teetering on the edge of insanity at all times. I can't stand most artists, although Aidan is an exception. And he's very good, too, I have to admit that. Those life masks he makes are interesting. He'll want to do one of you. Me, I only date athletes. No artists. That's my rule. So," she added generously, "you can have Aidan. Just remember, I warned you. He's half-mad, like the rest of us. I hope you know what you're doing."

Although Rachel laughed again, she would remember Paloma's warning later. It would come back to haunt her.

When they returned to the group, Bibi was gone.

"Where's my roommate?" Rachel asked Joseph, although she already had a pretty good idea.

Joseph tilted his head in the direction of the door. "She left. With that Samms guy. The waiter? The one with the dark, brooding look. I heard the theater department is doing *Dracula* next year. They should speak to him about playing the lead."

"Dracula isn't dark and brooding," Rachel disagreed. "He's pale and vapid."

"You're personally acquainted with him?" Joseph snapped.

Rachel glanced at Paloma, who pointedly raised smoothly arched, heavily pencilled dark brows, as if to say, See? What did I tell you? Hypersensitive! Next time, pay attention when I talk about artists.

The crowd had thinned, and Rachel could see through the glass door that darkness had fallen. She was reluctant to walk across campus alone, and was relieved when Aidan said, "Why don't we all go over to Vinnie's for pizza? Rachel? Come with us?"

She liked the way he said that. Casually. As if he didn't know that he was rescuing her from a solitary walk back to the dorm. As if he really wanted her to come along if she had the time.

She had the time.

They were about to leave when a very pretty girl in jeans and a tank top approached, wrestling with a large, and clearly heavy, canvas.

Both Aidan and Joseph ran to help, taking her burden from her.

"Oh, thanks," she gasped, laughing, "you guys are lifesavers. I'm taking this to my car . . . or was it taking me? I'm not sure. Anyway, if you wouldn't mind, I'd really appreciate some help. My car's right out front."

They obliged, leading the way out of the building. The girl followed.

Paloma touched Rachel's elbow, halting her. "That's Samantha Widdoes," she said in a low voice. "She's one of *us*. She's not very good, but she doesn't seem to care. She says she loves painting and that's all that counts. She's rich, so I guess she can afford to think that way. The rest of us have to think about whether we're going to earn a living or not."

"Maybe she did the seascape," Rachel said aloud. "You know, the one at the end of the far wall?"

"Oh, that thing. No, she doesn't work much in oil. Tried it once, and made a terrible mess. She knows her limitations. Most of her work is with pastels. She does trees, bushes, sky, water, flowery kinds of things that the guys make fun of. They'd never sell, but I think they're romantic."

So Samantha Widdoes, Artist, was pretty and rich, but not terribly talented, and didn't care all that much. She was, Rachel saw now, standing beside the car smiling up at Aidan, who looked interested. Very interested. But then, so did Joseph, who was also standing beside Samantha, glowering at Aidan.

"Guys," Paloma said in disgust as they approached the car, "they're all the same. All it takes is a pretty face, a great body, wealth, perfect teeth, and they're falling all over themselves. So who needs talent?"

Rachel laughed. The comment was just what she needed to stifle her jealousy. And she was glad it had, because Samantha turned out to be nice. Very friendly, smiling and shaking hands when she was introduced to Rachel.

"How did you like the exhibit?" she asked pleasantly.

"Loved it. By the way," Rachel said hurriedly, "do you by any chance know who painted the seascape?"

Joseph and Aidan groaned. "Not that again!" Joseph cried. "Do you often suffer from these morbid fixations?"

"Seascape?" Samantha asked, furrowing pale brows over deep brown eyes. "I don't remember that one. Actually, I didn't get much of a chance to view tonight. I was busy helping set things up, and then I got trapped in a corner with Dr. Lewis from art history. But," she added thoughtfully, "I don't remember anyone in class ever working on a seascape." She looked at Rachel. "Why? Did you like the painting?"

"It's not that Rachel liked it," Joseph interjected dryly, "it's just that she thinks she sees someone drowning in the painting. No one else sees it, of course, but that's because it's not there. It's just a lot of blue and green vomit, that's all. Can't imagine why anyone would even have the gall to hang it."

"Joseph," Samantha scolded mildly, "you know better than to tell people how to interpret paintings." To Rachel, she said, "Do you often see things in paintings that no one else sees? How fascinating."

"No. I don't. I guess it was an optical illusion or something."

"Well, you might want to check the canvas again. Some artists put their initials on the back of the canvas, instead of the front," Samantha explained. "You might check. Then you could always ask the artist."

"Thanks," Rachel said, nodding. "Maybe I will."

"You're not going to let go of this, are you?" Aidan asked as they climbed into the car.

"Maybe I will," Rachel said lightly, "and maybe I won't. I haven't decided yet."

"Well, in the meantime," Aidan said, smiling, "can we please go to Vinnie's? I'm not ready to be a starving artist. Not just yet."

Chapter 2

"The masks are fun," Aidan said around a mouthful of pizza, "and they're what I do best. I tried oils and watercolors and pastels, but then I came across the life masks and knew that was something I could really sink my teeth into. Three of mine are hanging in the lobby. Did you see them?"

Rachel shook her head. She'd been too fixated on the seascape. "I'll look at them tomorrow. So, how do you make the masks?"

"It's easy."

Joseph hooted. "Oh, yeah, right, McKay. Easy for you." To Rachel, he said, "I gave it up. Tried half a dozen times. Made such a mess, I almost got tossed out of class. Aidan's being modest. Totally out of character for him, by the way. Must be trying to impress you."

"I am," Aidan said. "So don't ruin it, okay? Anyway," he hunched forward, elbows on the

Formica table, his eyes bright, "say you were the subject — and I really hope you'll let me do one of you — you'd lie on a table with a cardboard tray under your head to catch any spills, and I'd coat your face and hairline with grease so the mask wouldn't stick. Then I'd mix up the plaster, put straws in your nose so you could breathe, you'd close your eyes, and I'd pour the plaster over your face."

Rachel gasped. "Not my face, you wouldn't! Are you serious? People let you do that to them?"

"Well, it's not like they can't breathe, Rachel." Aidan looked disappointed at her reaction. "Don't forget about the straws. And it doesn't take long for the plaster to harden. When I pull it off, I have a perfect mask of that person's face."

"*You* do," Joseph groused. "Not me. Mine never harden properly or they harden too fast, or the nose is sloppy. Once, I didn't put enough petroleum jelly on a girl's hairline before I poured the plaster. When I tried to take the mask off, her bangs were stuck. I had to cut them free with an X-Acto knife, or she'd have been walking around with a plaster mask on her face for the rest of her life. She was *not* a happy camper."

Paloma laughed. "She had the weirdest-looking hair on campus for a couple of weeks."

"Why would someone let you do that?" Rachel asked Aidan. "Cover their face with plaster? It sounds so horrible."

Annoyance was very visible on Aidan's face. "It's *art*, Rachel. They do it for art."

"And out of vanity," Paloma said dryly. "You'd be surprised at how many people are willing, even eager, to be immortalized in plaster."

"You *are* going to let me do a life mask of you, aren't you, Rachel?" Aidan asked. "Those cheekbones deserve to be cast in plaster for all the world to see."

"They can see them just fine, right here on my face," Rachel. She didn't want to make Aidan mad so soon in their relationship, if indeed he was interested in a relationship. But letting someone pour plaster over her face would take the kind of complete trust that Rachel wasn't sure she was capable of.

Changing the subject, she said, "So anyway, where do you work? I know it's in the Fine Arts building, but where?"

"On the tenth floor. It's all studios. So are eight and nine. But I like the tenth. The light is better."

"You lug bags of plaster up ten flights of

stairs?" No wonder he looked like he worked out regularly.

Aidan shook his head. "There's a dumb-waiter in the lobby. We just stick our stuff in there and haul it on upstairs with the pulley ropes."

Rachel was relieved Aidan had stopped pressing her about modelling for one of his masks. But she knew he'd ask again. He seemed determined.

On their way out of Vinnie's, they met Bibi, holding Rudy Samm's hand and smiling. Unlike Rudy, who barely nodded as they passed in the entryway.

What a creepy guy, Rachel thought. I myself wouldn't want to run into him in a dark alley.

Aidan walked her back to Lester. Before they parted she promised that she would return to the art exhibit the next day, Saturday, and view his life masks.

"See you there," he said, and turned to leave. But as he walked away, he called over his shoulder, "Think about doing one, okay? I'm ready whenever you are."

By that time, Rachel thought as she went inside, we'll both be old and gray and any mask of me will be full of wrinkles.

It had been a good day, and she was tired.

Knowing Bibi wouldn't be home until late, Rachel showered and went to bed. She was asleep before she had time to do as Aidan had asked and think about the mask.

The young man in jeans and white T-shirt standing on the riverbank above the waterfall is tall and thin, with thick, windblown hair the color of carrots. His back and shoulders bend slightly over the fishing rod gripped firmly in his hands, and at his feet lies an open textbook. His eyes alternate between the textbook page and the fishing rod to see if he has a bite. He reads a little, then glances up to see if he's got a bite, then reads a few more sentences before checking the rod again.

He is situated closer to the waterfall than he's ever been. Dangerous, someone has warned him, but Ted Leonides seldom pays attention to warnings of that sort. They are so like the ones his mother had given him repeatedly when he was little: "Don't climb that tree, you'll fall and break your neck," "Wear your raincoat or you'll catch pneumonia in this weather," "Stay away from that old abandoned house or you'll fall through the floorboards and break a leg." He has never fallen out of a tree, never caught pneumonia, never broken a leg. Now, when people warn him

*away from things, he feels perversely drawn
toward those things, trying to prove something.
He isn't sure to whom. His mother has been
dead for eight years, so it couldn't be her.*

*Himself, maybe. Maybe he's trying to prove
something to himself.*

*The forest surrounding this part of the riv-
erbank is peaceful and quiet. No one ever
comes up this far. The students at Salem University have been warned against the river in
the spring and fall when seasonal rains trans-
form the usually quiet, gentle waterfall into a
thundering torrent lunging over the outcrop-
ping of rock into a raging whirlpool at the
bottom.*

*The fisherman lifts his head from the text-
book pages to stare across the wild river to the
other side, where the riverbank rises up into a
steep, heavily wooded hill. It looks pretty over
there. Maybe, when he's memorized the eigh-
teenth chapter in his physics book in preparation for a quiz the following day, and given
up trying to catch anything in this wild and
muddy water, he'll walk back to the old rail-
road bridge behind campus and trek across it
to the other side, to do some exploring.*

*The bridge, too, is forbidden. Hasn't been
used in years. The metal supports are rusted
and full of holes, the wooden cross ties rotting*

as if giant insects have been chewing on them.

But he doesn't weigh very much. Not going to bring down an entire bridge just walking across it. And it sure does look pretty on the other side of the river.

He glances up at the sky. Looks like rain. Good fishing weather, but if he hangs around and waits for the rain, he'll never get across the bridge to take a look.

Deciding, he lays the fishing rod aside and bends to pick up his textbook.

He never sees the figure that darts out of the woods, and straight at him from behind. Its hands are raised high in the air and hold an object . . . long, wooden, with a smooth, rounded end . . . a baseball bat.

The figure, clothed in a long, black, flowing garment with a loose hood, swings the wooden object with both hands, connecting with the back of Ted Leonides's skull.

He doesn't make a sound. His body flies up and out, seeming to hang suspended in the air over the swollen river for long minutes before descending rapidly, limp as a rag doll, into the muddy, rushing water.

When he surfaces again, he is conscious, revived perhaps by the cold water. His eyes are wide with fear. His arms flail helplessly against the powerful current. His mouth is open in a silent scream of terror.

That raw, open horror in his face is because Ted Leonides knows he is being swept straight toward the waterfall that plunges to the rocks below.

And he knows there is nothing he can do to stop his helpless rush toward certain death.

He is right.

It takes only minutes.

The figure in black on the riverbank, the bat dangling from its left hand, watches in satisfied silence as the young fisherman is swept away, arms still flailing, his mouth still open in a scream silenced by the muddy water pouring into it.

As he is ripped backward toward the waterfall, his attacker tosses the bloody bat into the water. Then he turns and hurries along the riverbank to watch. He arrives at Lookout Point, the top of the hill where visitors come to view the waterfall, at the precise moment when the now-unconscious body is swept over the crest of the falls, spiralling down, down, amid the roar and rumble of the water, into the raging whirlpool and the jagged rocks below.

This time, Ted Leonides doesn't resurface.

He is gone.

The figure in black turns and hurries away,

*disappearing into the woods like a black
shadow erased by the sun.*

Rachel awoke soaked with sweat and shaking so violently, the headboard of her bed was knocking against the wall.

"What's going on?" Bibi muttered. But she didn't awaken. When Rachel didn't answer, because shock and fear had rendered her incapable of speech, Bibi rolled over and fell silent again.

Rachel shrank back against the wall, clutching the bedding to her chest. Her body was icy with sweat, her teeth chattering, her eyes as wide with terror as the eyes of the drowning victim.

She knew that fisherman. Ted Leonides, from math. Tall, quiet in class, but she'd thought she'd noticed an adventurous look in his eyes.

Why had she been dreaming about Ted Leonides? She hardly knew him.

Rachel sat up, still trembling violently. She drew a tissue from the box on her night table and wiped her face with it. Her long nightshirt was soaked with sweat, and she was freezing, in spite of the mild breeze coming in through the window. She glanced at the illuminated alarm clock beside the tissue box. Five-thirty

A.M. Campus was still dark, everyone else sensibly asleep.

Only Rachel Seaver sat on the edge of her bed trembling and sick and frightened because of a bad dream.

On shaky legs, she got up to change into a dry nightshirt, trying to still her thundering heart. It was only a dream, she told herself, as her grandmother would have done, and it's over. You're awake now, and there's nothing to be afraid of.

When she had changed into dry clothing, she crawled back into bed. But the dry T-shirt did nothing to warm her insides, which were still icy with fear.

It had been so *real*, that nightmare. Unlike any she'd ever had before. And she'd had many, when she was young. After the sudden, shocking death of her parents in a taxicab accident while on vacation, she had moved into her grandmother's big old, Victorian house. It was full of dark nooks and crannies and strange, unsettling sounds. Sleeping in the huge, drafty, second-floor bedroom at the end of a dark hallway, Rachel had suffered for a long time from night terrors that had kept her grandmother, who was wrestling with her own grief, up night after night.

It had nearly undone both of them.

But they'd got through it and come out on the other side, and after a very long time, the night terrors had ended.

Until tonight.

Again she wondered why she had been dreaming about Ted Leonides.

Rachel had never seen anyone die, except on television and in the movies. She tried to tell herself that the nightmare was exactly the same thing. A dream was every bit as unreal as anything on film. More so, because at least on film, there actually were real people, actors, doing and saying what you were seeing. In a dream, not even that much was real.

Telling herself that didn't help. Because dream or not, she had *seen* Ted die. He had been hit on the back of the head by a horrible creature all in black, he had flown out over the water and then into it, and then she had watched him descend over the waterfall and onto the rocks below. She had seen the shock, the terror in his eyes, seen it as clearly as if she'd been standing on the riverbank as it happened.

So it really was as if she *had seen* someone die.

And he hadn't died accidentally. That made it so much worse. He hadn't just died, like someone who'd been sick for a long time, or, like her parents, in a car wreck. Someone had *made* it happen. Someone had *killed* him.

Huddled deep within her blankets, Rachel shuddered again.

That was when she remembered the painting, as if the shudder had shaken the sight of it back into her mind. The painting. The seascape at the exhibit. The drowning figure no one else had seen. In the painting, the figure's arms were flailing, just as Ted's had been in her nightmare. The eyes in the painting had been wide with fear, like his in her dream, the mouth open in that same terrible, silent scream.

The painting. Was *that* why she'd had the nightmare? Because of that painting and what she thought she'd seen within its strokes of vivid green and brilliant blue?

Rachel latched on to the thought as a possible, reasonable explanation for the nightmare. An explanation that made sense. Except . . . except that it didn't explain why she had seen Ted Leonides in her dream. Why not someone she knew better? Or someone who had disagreed with her about what was in the painting, like that rude waiter? That would make more sense.

Maybe dreams weren't supposed to make sense.

She lay there, eyes wide open, for a long time, trying to forget the nightmare, until a pale, silvery dawn crept in through the wide window.

Finally, she drifted back into sleep. When she awoke a second time, the sun lit up the room and her digital clock read eight forty-five. Saturday morning. No classes for her. Rachel rolled over and would have returned to sleep if the door hadn't opened to let Bibi in, armed with two steaming cups of coffee. She kicked the door closed behind her, but instead of bringing Rachel the coffee, she said in an odd voice, "Rachel," and then backed up to her own bed and sank down on it as if her legs would no longer support her.

Rachel pulled herself to a sitting position. Bibi's cheeks were the same off-white as the wall behind her, and her eyes looked slightly glazed as she stared at her roommate. "Rachel?" she said again.

"Bibi, what's wrong?"

Bibi's large blue eyes moved to Rachel's face. "You know that guy Ted Leonides?" she asked.

Rachel's heart stopped beating.

Because she didn't answer, Bibi mistook her silence for an inability to identify Ted Leonides. "The tall skinny redhead we see heading for the river sometimes with a fishing pole, remember?"

Rachel struggled to find her voice. She finally managed to choke out, "What about him? What about Ted Leonides?"

Bibi's voice, when it came, seemed to Rachel to be miles and miles away, as if Bibi were trying to tell her something from the opposite end of a long, dark tunnel.

"He's dead, Rachel. He went fishing last night, and he fell over the waterfall and drowned in the pool at the bottom."

Chapter 3

Silence fell over the room as Rachel tried desperately to reject what she thought she'd heard Bibi say. Bibi couldn't have said that. Not possible. Too awful to even consider.

It's just the nightmare, she told herself firmly. I wasn't quite awake when Bibi came into the room and I was still thinking about that horrible dream, so I imagined that she said Ted was dead. But, of course, she couldn't have.

And then Bibi said it again. "Rachel?" she said, leaning forward slightly on her bed, the two cups of coffee still in her hands. "Did you hear what I said? Ted Leonides is dead. Drowned. Why don't you say something?"

From some faraway place where Bibi's words couldn't reach her, Rachel wondered idly why Bibi was still holding onto those coffee cups. Weren't they hot? Why wasn't she burning her fingers on them?

Oh, of course. This was still part of the dream and so Bibi's fingers weren't burning because none of this was real.

"Rachel, you're scaring me! *Say* something, or I'm going to go get our R.A."

Still Rachel said nothing. She sat frozen and silent on her bed, her face drained of color, her eyes glazed, the bedding clutched to her chest.

Bibi waited a few more minutes. When she continued to get no response from her roommate, she jumped up, deposited the coffee cups on a small table, and ran from the room.

She was back a few minutes later with a sturdy, dark-haired girl in tow. "You have to do something," Bibi was saying to their resident advisor, Carmella Diaz, as the two entered the room. "All I did was tell her Ted Leonides drowned last night. I don't understand why she's taking it like this. We hardly knew him."

The R.A. sat on the edge of Rachel's bed. "Rachel, snap out of it!" she said crisply, gently shaking Rachel's right shoulder.

Rachel's head swivelled slightly, and she stared blankly at Carmella as if she'd never seen her before. Then, very slowly, her eyes cleared, and when she opened her mouth, she said quietly, "It's not true, is it? Ted isn't really dead, is he?"

"Yes. And I know it's horrible, it really is. Everyone's in shock. But Bibi said you hardly knew him, Rachel. Why are you taking it so hard?"

Rachel's mind was working again. She knew she couldn't tell them about the dream. If she said aloud, "Because I *saw* it happen, all of it, every single, sickening minute of it," Carmella and Bibi would cart her off to the loony bin.

Rachel reacted as she always did when she wasn't sure what to do. She became defensive. "Why shouldn't I take it hard?" she cried. "Someone was killed last night!" She realized as soon as she said it that she shouldn't have said "killed." Bibi had made Ted's death sound accidental.

"I mean," she hastily amended, "someone *died* last night. It's horrible. So I don't think I overreacted at all."

"Yes, you did," Bibi said. "You acted as if your best friend had died."

Rachel shuddered. "No, I didn't. It's just that Ted is . . . was . . . in one of my classes and I liked him. You walked in and said he was dead, just like that, without any warning at all." She glared at Bibi. "It's a good thing you're not planning to go into medicine. I can't imagine you breaking bad news to your patients' relatives."

Bibi, her natural color restored to her face, nodded ruefully. "You're right. I'm sorry. You know me. I just sort of let things spill out of my mouth and hope they'll come out the right way. I guess this one didn't. But," she added in her own defense, "I've never had to tell anyone something so horrible before. How was I supposed to know the right way to do it?" She handed Rachel one of the cups and, taking the other over to her own bed, said, "I am sorry, though, Rachel." She sat down and sipped thoughtfully. "I guess hearing it that way was pretty awful for you."

Seeing it was even worse, Rachel thought, feeling sick. She wanted to tell them what she'd seen in her nightmare. But she didn't dare. How could she possibly explain that she'd seen something in a dream before it had actually happened?

And anyway, it couldn't have happened exactly the way she'd seen it, she told herself as the hot coffee began to warm her. What happened to Ted was an accident. A simple, *horrible* accident. He'd slipped on the muddy riverbank and fallen in, been swept over the waterfall. The detailed scene she'd witnessed in her nightmare was just a bizarre coincidence.

Very bizarre.

The whole thing was bizarre. And horrible. Yesterday, Ted had been very much alive. She had seen him loping across campus with an armload of books. No fishing pole. He must have gone to the river after his classes were over for the day. And now, not even twenty-four hours later, he was dead.

Dead. Drowned, just as she'd seen in the nightmare.

Satisfied that Rachel was herself again, Carmella got up to leave.

"Did anyone see it happen?" Rachel asked suddenly, unable to stop herself. "Ted's accident? Did someone see it?"

Carmella shook her head. "No, I don't think so. Two guys biking along the river path found him this morning, floating facedown in one of the eddies. His shirt was caught on a branch, I guess, or he would have been long gone, with the current the way it is now."

When she had gone, Rachel drank the last of her coffee. She needed to tell someone about the nightmare. Her chest ached with the weight of it.

But who could she tell?

Not Bibi. Bibi Jensen was a no-nonsense

farm girl who believed firmly that the only way to cope with life was to meet it head-on, without illusions. She was proud of saying she had never believed in Santa Claus, had never read a fairy tale in her life or had a daydream, wasn't the tiniest bit superstitious and had no faith in signs or omens or dreams of any sort, good or bad.

Bibi would dismiss Rachel's nightmare as swiftly as she'd flick a piece of lint off her navy-blue sweater.

The police, then? Rachel slipped out of bed and began to dress in jeans and a Salem University sweatshirt over a white T-shirt. Should she go to the police? If they were convinced that Ted's death had been accidental, would they even bother with an investigation?

Not on the basis of someone's nightmare, they wouldn't.

The thought of walking into the Twin Falls police station or the campus security office and saying, "I had this dream . . ." made Rachel want to laugh aloud.

It was a nightmare, Rachel, she told herself firmly, and that's *all* it was. You do not have ESP. Get over it.

Getting outside helped. On a beautiful Saturday morning in spring, campus was alive with joggers and bikers, runners, and students hurrying to and from classes. Carmella had said that everyone was in shock about Ted's death, but it didn't seem so to Rachel. Although there were some white faces and eyes wide with disbelief, life seemed to be going on as usual.

Rachel found herself very annoyed that people were doing *normal* things when something so *abnormal* had happened the night before. It seemed to her that the nightmare . . . so real, so vivid . . . had created a bond between her and Ted that had never been there while he was alive.

Rachel felt overcome by a strange need to find out exactly what had happened up there near the falls. She didn't want to go near the place, but she found herself unwillingly striking out in that direction.

She would have kept going if someone hadn't called out her name.

It was Aidan, running toward her from the art building, his long, dark hair tied back in a ponytail, his T-shirt and jeans smeared with daubs of gold and rust paint. "Hey, how's it going?" he said, a little short of breath as he caught up with her. "I've been working on some backdrops for the drama department. Where are you headed?"

"Nowhere," she said quickly. She hadn't actually been going up to the falls, had she? What an insane idea! The last thing she wanted to see this morning was the scene in her nightmare. It would bring it all back, when what she really wanted to do was forget it.

"Here, come sit on the fountain for a sec," he said, throwing himself down on the low, stone wall around the fountain in the center of the Commons. Because of the unusually mild weather, there were students lying on blankets all across the level green, some studying, some talking, some just working on a tan.

"They don't act like someone was killed last night," Rachel said with more than a hint of resentment in her voice. Shouldn't campus look different this morning than it usually did? Shouldn't *something* have changed? "I mean, died. Someone died."

"You heard about Ted. Maybe some of them don't know yet."

"News like that spreads quickly, Aidan. Of course they've heard. But," she added, glancing around the Commons, "they act as if they don't care."

"Well, Ted was a nice guy," Aidan said, "but I don't think he had that many friends. Kept to himself pretty much." He glanced over at her, mild curiosity in his eyes. "Were you a friend of his? Is that why you're upset?"

Rachel bristled. What on earth was *wrong*

with people? Did you have to know someone personally and well before you could care that they'd died? Ted Leonides was only eighteen years old! "No, I didn't know him very well. But what difference does it make? He shouldn't be *dead*, should he? It's all wrong."

"I agree," Aidan said, nodding. "But maybe everyone's afraid that if they show how they feel, they won't look cool. When I was in tenth grade, a good friend of mine died. A bunch of guys were out hiking, and this guy, Andrew, fell down a deserted mine shaft. Broke his neck. It was really rough at school for a while after that, because we all felt sick and mad and you can't let any of that stuff show when you're sixteen. So we all got stomachaches and headaches and couldn't sleep and our grades sank, but we never once talked about it, any of us. We never admitted out loud that Andrew's death had got to us. Afraid it would make us look soft or something, I guess. Who knows? Anyway, that's probably the way a lot of people feel right now."

"Well, that's stupid," Rachel said heatedly.

Aidan shrugged. "Maybe. But that's the way it is."

"Were you with them? On the hike?"

He shook his head. "I was supposed to be. But I'd broken curfew the night before, my old man caught me, and I spent all day Saturday cleaning out the garage. Maybe one of the reasons I had nightmares for a while after that was knowing that if I'd been with them, I probably would have been in the lead. I usually was. Always in a hurry, that's me. So I could have been the first one to dive down that mine shaft instead of Andrew." He shook his head, his mouth grim. "I thought about that a lot after he died. Almost felt guilty because it was him instead of me. Weird."

Maybe, Rachel thought. But having a nightmare after a horrible accident happened wasn't nearly as weird as having one *before* it happened. How could you dream about something that hadn't even happened yet?

"You're shaking," Aidan said suddenly, surprise in his voice. "Are you that upset about Ted?"

Rachel stood up. "I want to see that painting again," she said, her voice steady.

"What painting?"

"The seascape. The one at the exhibit yesterday. The painting that I thought showed someone drowning and none of the rest of you did, remember?"

Aidan stood up, nodding. "Yeah, I remember. It wasn't very good."

"Maybe not," Rachel said crisply, turning on

her heel to move toward the Fine Arts building. "But *someone* did drown last night. So I want to see that painting again."

She moved swiftly across campus, Aidan matching her stride for stride. "Rachel, you really think that painting is connected to what happened to Ted? That's crazy!"

She ignored him.

Taking the hint, he fell silent. But he stayed with her.

The art building was even more crowded than it had been the night before, although the bulk of the crowd seemed to be adults. Some Rachel recognized as professors. Others were, she decided, residents of Twin Falls and other neighboring communities. From the sound of their voices, they seemed to approve of most of the work on display.

But there was, like yesterday, no crowd in front of the far wall.

Rachel knew the exact spot where the seascape was hanging. She pushed her way through the crowd, anxious to see if her eyes had been lying to her. Maybe this time she would see the painting exactly as everyone else had, and know that Aidan was right. That there was no connection between the seascape and Ted's death.

Elbowing her way through a thick cluster of

people discussing the pros and cons of a work of sculpture in the center of the room, Rachel emerged on the other side of the group and aimed straight for the far wall.

When she was still several feet away the crowd cleared, and her eyes went to the spot where the seascape had been hanging.

She stopped, her mouth dropping open in disappointment.

It was gone.

Chapter 4

Rachel stared questioningly at the blank space on the wall where the seascape had, just the night before, been hanging. "It's gone," she said. "The exhibit isn't over until tomorrow. Why would someone take their work down already?"

"The artist probably hated it as much as everyone else did," Aidan said.

Rachel barely heard him. She was studying the blank space on the wall almost as intently as she'd studied the painting. "Now I'll never know who painted it," she complained.

"Look, here's what probably happened," Aidan said seriously. "We were told six months ago there'd be an exhibit this weekend, so most of us moved our butts trying to get as much decent work done as possible. But the seascape artist, if we can call him that, probably goofed off until it was too late — then panicked and dug up an old work that only a truly desperate person would dare to hang in public. When he saw how people reacted to it, he had the smarts to take it down. We can only hope he destroyed it completely."

"I don't care what you say, the painting wasn't that bad," Rachel said coolly, turning away from him.

Aidan laughed. "You mean, you don't know much about art, but you know what you like? I never thought I'd actually hear someone say that."

Rachel's mouth tightened. He was insufferable. Did she really want to get to know someone who talked to her as if she belonged in a kindergarten finger-painting class? "I wanted to see the painting because I still think I saw someone drowning in it, and someone *did* drown last night, in case you've forgotten," she said stiffly. "That has to seem a bit weird, even to you. And now the painting is gone. So I can't check it out again."

"You didn't see anybody drowning in that painting," he said firmly. "And neither did anyone else. Come and have breakfast with me and I'll teach you everything I know about art."

"That shouldn't take long," Rachel snapped.

Aidan's face reddened. "Ouch! I guess I had that coming. Sorry. Just showing off, I guess, trying to impress. Not usually my style. I can see why now, because it doesn't seem to be working, does it?"

"No, it doesn't." Rachel glanced around the lobby. The crowd had thinned, and she could see the other paintings clearly. "All of the other works have names under them. The seascape didn't." She aimed a glance at Aidan. "Can't you at least admit it's odd that there was no name tag under that one painting?"

"No. I wouldn't want *my* name under it, either. Can we please go eat?"

She wasn't going to learn any more about the seascape by staring at a blank wall. He *had* apologized, and she *was* hungry.

But before she turned away, she saw the painting again as clearly as if it were still hanging there, the blues, the greens, the wild water, the blobs of pinkish paint that she'd taken for arms and a face — especially the face, eyes and mouth wide open in terror. And on the heels of that repugnant vision came the nightmare, flooding back into her mind in vivid detail, the fisherman on the bank, the shadowy figure darting out of the woods with the baseball bat, sending the startled victim flying out into the brown rushing water and over the falls. . . .

Rachel shuddered violently.

"Hey, what's going on?" Aidan said with concern, reaching out with one arm as if to prop her up. "Are you sick?"

If she shared the nightmare with him, how would he react? She didn't know him well enough yet to guess, and she wasn't ready to risk ridicule. "Of course I'm not sick," she said, brushing his arm away. "Just hungry. Let's go eat."

"Looking for the seascape?" a voice said from behind them.

They turned around. Rudy Samms, a broom and dustpan in his hand, nodded at them. "Someone took it down during the night."

"During the night?" Rachel echoed. "How do you know that?"

"Because it was here last night when I came back to clean up. I was the last one to leave the building, and that painting was still here then. But it wasn't here when I came in, first thing this morning," Rudy finished. "So I knew someone had to have taken it during the night."

"Don't you lock up when you leave?"

Rudy glowered at Rachel from beneath dark brows. "That's a stupid question. Of course I lock up. But other people have keys. All of the art professors have them, and some of the students do, too. There are studios upstairs, and sometimes they need to get in to work."

"I *told* you, Rachel," Aidan said, "the artist was probably embarrassed by the painting and removed it."

"In the middle of the night?" Rachel asked sarcastically.

"On the other hand," Aidan added, "maybe the artist decided to take it down, lug it back upstairs, and put it away in the storage closet, that infamous graveyard of Paintings Not Worth The Nail To Hang Them On. In which case, it could still be in the dumbwaiter, waiting to be transported up." Taking Rachel's hand, he led her to a small door, half Rachel's size, cut into the wall near the entrance to the building.

He opened the door and Rachel peeked inside. The dumbwaiter was really just a wooden cupboard hung on ropes in a pulley arrangement, "It's like a mini-elevator," she commented. "What's it for?"

"For getting supplies and artwork up to the studios on the upper floors." Aidan closed the small door. "Not a bad workout, hauling twenty-five pound bags of plaster up to the tenth floor. But there are times when I wish this thing was automated, like the elevator."

Even as he said that, the elevator door opened and Joseph, Paloma, and Samantha stepped out, laughing. Joseph and Samantha were wearing paint-daubed shorts, like Aidan, and tank tops. Paloma was dressed in a long, black-flowered dress and black high-buttoned shoes. A small, black velvet hat sat on her head, the lacy veil draped over her eyes. All three were carrying huge, black, art portfolios.

"I see your favorite painting has disappeared," Joseph said to Rachel.

"I don't want to talk about it," Rachel said curtly. "We're going to breakfast. You can all come if you promise not to discuss art."

Samantha, looking very pretty, her blonde hair piled carelessly on top of her head, laughed. "But Rachel, what else is there?" She smiled at Aidan. "Aidan, haven't you indoctrinated this girl yet?"

"I've been trying. It's not easy. She has a mind of her own when it comes to art, and, I suspect, just about everything else."

"I would love it," Rachel said, her voice as smooth as glass, "if you wouldn't discuss me as if I weren't here."

Aidan stiffened, but Samantha laughed again and said, "Sorry. We'd love to go to breakfast. We've been slaving upstairs since the wee, small hours of the morning, and we're all starved."

They were almost to the door when Rachel spied a small painting hanging in a dim corner.

What caught her attention first was the size of the work. It was noticeably smaller than others surrounding it. Then, as she glanced at it, she was attracted by its colors. Without saying anything to anyone, she wandered over to take a closer look.

The work was a still life — flowers in a vase — painted in soft, muted lilacs, pinks, and pale blues. She liked the painting, and said so, aloud.

"You're not serious," Joseph said, moving to stand at her side. "It's so trite!"

"I *do* like it," Rachel cried, "and I really don't care whether you approve or not, Joseph."

There was an awkward silence behind them, where Aidan, Paloma, and Samantha were standing.

Then Samantha said, "Well, good for you, Rachel. Joseph thinks he's Salem's art expert. Of course you can like anything you want. Actually, I think that one's pretty, too. I love the way the artist used the mauve. Gives it a lot of power."

Rachel was about to turn away when something else caught her eye. Viewed from the side, there seemed to be something different about the vase. It was, at first glance, just a dove-gray, urn-shaped container. That was what she had first seen and that was what she wanted to continue seeing.

But there was no mistaking the fact that the thick swirls and whorls on the vase seemed now to be creating a . . . a head . . . there the eyes, there the nose, and there the mouth, open, wide open, like the mouth in the seascape, in a scream of terror.

Rachel moaned softly to herself. Not again, no, please . . .

She took two steps sideways. An optical illusion, she urged silently, that's all it is. The paint had been applied in thick, broad strokes that overlapped each other, and she told herself those strokes were creating the effect that had caught her eye. She told herself that there wasn't really anything unusual there.

It's just a vase, she commanded, so don't do this again. Don't see something that no one else sees.

And they didn't see it, she could tell. Joseph was yawning with boredom, Aidan and Samantha were talking quietly, and Paloma was fiddling with the catch on her portfolio. None of them was the least bit interested in the still life.

Rachel would have given up then. She would have put the painting out of her mind and left to eat a perfectly normal breakfast. But as her head swivelled away from the painting, she noticed the lines. Beginning just beneath the "head" and continuing on down the front of the vase, she saw now a series of horizontal lines, equidistant from each other. She noticed them because they were so precise, so even, so straight, in a painting that seemed otherwise composed of semicircular strokes and swirls.

She stared at the lines. They *had* to be part of the design on the vase. Because how could they possibly be what they looked like to her?

What would a staircase be doing in a floral life?

Time to get your eyes checked, Rachel, she told herself, turning away from the painting. Then, remembering the nightmare about Ted, she added, and maybe your head at the same time.

"Rachel, come on!" Paloma whined.

But Rachel didn't move. There, off to the left side of the vase, midway down the series of lines, couldn't those two darker blue blobs be legs? That was what they looked like to her. Legs splayed out at angles, as if they were . . . as if they were falling? Falling down the stairs? Was that why the mouth was screaming?

Do *not* do this! Rachel cried silently, her

breath coming rapidly in her chest. You are deliberately trying to find some hidden, mysterious message in this stupid painting, just so you can convince yourself you weren't wrong about the seascape.

Rachel took another two steps away from the painting, walking backward. She bumped into Aidan's chest and turned toward him to apologize. "Let's go eat," she said, trying to collect herself and calm down.

But she couldn't stop the thoughts buzzing in her head. She had seen something sinister in the first painting. And look what had happened to Ted. Now she was seeing another strange image hidden in the still life. Someone falling down a flight of stairs.

She didn't *want* to see that. She wanted to see what everyone else saw, an ordinary and, according to Joseph, not great, painting of a vase of flowers. She wanted that more than anything.

But when she glanced back at the still life one more time, she knew with painful certainty that what she was looking at was someone tumbling helplessly down a steep flight of stairs, screaming in terror.

Chapter 5

At breakfast in the small cafeteria in the basement of Lester dorm, Rachel struggled to force the image of the still life from her mind. Acting moody wasn't going to endear her to Aidan and his friends. Although she had other friends, she liked this new group. Joseph was arrogant, Aidan could be patronizing, Paloma was a bit of a flake, and Samantha was a little intimidating. But they were all so *interesting*, and Rachel didn't want them writing her off as a hopeless basket case.

She sipped quietly on her orange juice as she glanced around the table. What was she doing with these people? What did she have in common with them?

She had met Aidan at a movie in Devereaux's rec room just two nights ago. She'd gone with Bibi, but as always, after the movie Bibi had latched onto a good-looking soccer player and wandered off. Rachel had been standing in the doorway, waiting to see if Bibi was coming back, when someone behind her said, "I'm trying to figure out why you're standing there alone. Could be because your friends went off to get something to eat. Or maybe you had an argument with your date and sent him on his way. Or, and this would certainly be *my* choice, you're here alone."

Rachel turned toward the voice. It was his eyes she noticed first. The brightest blue, without a hint of gray or hazel. He was leaning against the door frame, smiling at her. She didn't notice the paint-stained jeans or the slight slump to his shoulders or the cleft in his chin until much later. All she saw was the smile. And, of course, the eyes.

"I'm here alone," she said simply.

And then she wasn't.

They had talked the night away, and discovered that they had nothing at all in common. He'd been raised in a big, noisy family, while she was an only child, orphaned early and raised by a quiet but loving grandmother. He lived in a city, Albany. She was from a town so small, she'd read every interesting book in the library by the time she was fourteen. She liked rock, he liked jazz. She loved strawberries and cantaloupe, asparagus and broccoli. He said fruits and vegetables were okay, but the best food on earth was marshmallow creme on peanut butter, a concoction Rachel couldn't imagine trying to swallow. He was a night person, often working on his art until two or three in the morning, and had deliberately scheduled most of his classes for later in the day so he could sleep until ten or eleven. She got cranky if she wasn't in bed by midnight.

And, of course, there was what Rachel thought of as "the art thing." It wasn't as if she didn't like art. She just didn't know much about it, while Aidan seemed to eat, breathe, and sleep it.

They should not have been attracted to one another.

But they were.

The following day on campus, she had met Joseph through Aidan, and that evening he had invited her to the art exhibit.

She had no idea why Aidan was interested in her, if he was. Right now, he seemed far more interested in Samantha, who was discussing not art, but music with him. They had the same tastes, while Rachel had never heard of the performers whose names they tossed around with easy familiarity.

She was feeling as left out as if they'd been discussing art, after all.

But she knew that wasn't the only thing bothering her. Try as she would, she couldn't completely erase the image of the screaming face on the staircase in the still life painting.

"You're awfully quiet," Aidan said suddenly. "Anything wrong, Rachel?"

They were all looking at her.

"I'm just anxious to get outside, that's all. It's such a great day. I hate to waste it."

The others agreed, and Rachel was happy to hear Samantha sigh and say regretfully that she had work to do at the art building. Joseph had errands to run, and Paloma was going into town to check out the jewelry displays in the only two jewelry stores in the small community of Twin Falls.

"Too bad you guys all have things to do," Rachel said, secretly pleased. If Aidan had no plans, she'd have him all to herself on this gorgeous spring day.

He had no plans.

Rachel never knew what possessed her, talking him into going to the waterfall with her. She hadn't intended to, hadn't even thought about going there. The whole idea of being with Aidan was to keep her mind off the seascape and Ted and the still life.

But they were walking across campus, past a raucous game of volleyball taking place on the Commons, when an irresistible urge to view the scene from her nightmare came over her and propelled her feet in that direction.

Puzzled, Aidan went with her.

She had no idea what she expected to find when they got there. Some sign, some clue that, as in her dream, there was more to Ted's accident that anyone suspected? Maybe the cruel baseball bat, buried in mud along the shore? A piece of black fabric from the cape hanging from a sapling branch at the edge of the woods? Footprints?

She saw none of those things. There was nothing there. Nothing but the worn, muddy path, the dense, sun-dappled woods on their right, the locomotivelike roar of the waterfall just up ahead, the hill rising up out of the water on the opposite shore.

Nothing unusual. It could have been a picture on a postcard.

"I don't know why I wanted to come here," she said to Aidan as they moved on toward Lookout Point. "Seems kind of morbid now. I mean, someone *was* killed here."

He turned on the path, stopped, and looked at her. "That's the second time you've said that."

Rachel stopped, too. "Said what?"

"That someone was *killed*. Everyone else

says Ted died. You say killed. How come?"

Rachel felt her cheeks growing warm. "I
. . . I don't know." She still didn't want to tell
him about the nightmare. Bad enough that he
thought she was an art ignoramus. She didn't
want him thinking she was a flake who believed
in dreams, too. "It's just . . . well, the fall *did*
kill him, didn't it? So he was killed, right?"

Aidan thought for a minute. "Oh, yeah, I
guess. But . . . when you said it, it sounded
like you meant it wasn't an accident."

Rachel felt as if Aidan's brilliant blue eyes
were seeing clear through to her soul. "Why
would I think that?" she asked lightly. "No one
else does." Then she added quickly, "Listen, I
don't want to be here, after all. It's creepy.
Can we just go? I feel like playing some volleyball; how about it?"

Although he agreed and followed her as she
retraced her steps along the path, away from
the roar of the waterfall, she could feel his eyes
on her back, and knew he was still puzzled.

"I'm very good at volleyball, by the way,"
she called over her shoulder as they emerged
from the path onto campus. "And I'll bet you've
been so busy painting pictures, you haven't had
time to perfect your game."

"Wrong," he said as he caught up with her
and grabbed her hand. "You're not one of those

57

people who think all artists are wimps, are you? Pale-faced and languid from starving in a garret? Because if you are, you're about to change your tune. I've been playing volleyball since I was eight. Two of my older brothers and I were in the regional semifinals. Didn't win, but we put up a good fight. So, if you're smart, you'll play on *my* team."

She did, and he was right. He was very good. So was she, and she got so caught up in the spirit of the game that all thoughts of screaming mouths and baseball bats and roaring waterfalls were swept completely from her mind. It didn't even bother her that one of the opposing teammates was Rudy Samms, who proved to be as poor a sport as he was ill-mannered, accusing the winners of stacking their team with the tallest people on campus.

"Maybe that's why he's so rude," Rachel mused as, sunburned and weary, she and Aidan made their way to Lester. "He's got a complex about being short."

Aidan laughed. "That's not his problem."

Rachel glanced up at him. "What is it, then? You sound like you know."

"He wants to be an artist. Trouble is, he doesn't have any talent. I haven't seen any of his work, but Samantha said when he applied here last spring, he was rejected by the dean of the art school. She said she heard the dean suggested that Samms take up engineering instead. I've seen him with a portfolio a couple of times, so he must still be working on stuff. And he hangs around the art building a lot, working as a waiter or custodian. I guess he's not ready to admit the dean was right."

"My roommate has a crush on him. I don't get it. They're not anything alike. Bibi is fun and smart and happy, most of the time."

Aidan laughed. "Yeah, well, you and I aren't anything alike, either. Doesn't seem to matter, does it?"

Rachel felt a glow of warmth. No, it didn't seem to matter.

"Gotta feel sorry for someone like Samms," Aidan said then. "Must be awful to want to do something, be something, and not have what it takes."

"I haven't decided yet what I want to do," Rachel admitted. "Everyone else seems to have plans, but not me. I don't have any special talent, like you and Joseph and the others."

He tugged on her hand to stop her in her tracks. He put his hands on her shoulders and smiled down at her. "Oh, yeah, you do," he said. And he bent his head and kissed her.

Rachel was flustered, caught off guard. But not so flustered that she didn't kiss him back.

They were interrupted when Bibi came hurrying out of the building. "Oh, Rachel," she said, barely pausing, "glad I caught you. You've got a package upstairs. A big one. I left it by your bed. I'm meeting Rudy. See you later." And she ran off.

"A package?" Rachel smiled. "My grandmother's snickerdoodles," she said, tugging on Aidan's hand. "The best cookies to ever come out of an oven. Come on, I'm feeling generous. I'll share. Your reward for playing a great game of volleyball and . . . other things."

Bibi had left the door to room 826 unlocked. "We hardly ever lock it," Rachel explained as she opened the door and gestured to Aidan to come in. "We can never find our keys. My grandmother would have a stroke if she knew how careless we are."

She glanced around the room for the package, expecting to find a brown-paper-wrapped shoebox on her bed. There was nothing on her bed except a red notebook and her nightshirt.

The package was on the floor, leaning against the bed. And Rachel remembered then, Bibi had said the package was big. She wouldn't have said that about a box of cookies.

The package *was* big. It was also flat and rectangular, wrapped in white plastic, and tied with twine.

"Is it your birthday?" Aidan asked as Rachel moved toward the package.

"No," she said, "it's not." There was something about the shape of the package, something familiar, something that birthed a tiny kernel of uneasiness in her chest. It *wasn't* her birthday, and she hadn't been expecting a package, and although her grandmother occasionally surprised her with a new sweater or a pair of gloves or thick athletic socks, she had never sent anything in so large a package.

Rachel unearthed a pair of scissors from a desk drawer and cut the twine. Slowly, carefully, she began to peel off the white plastic, beginning at the top. She did it slowly because she had already guessed, from the shape of the package, what was inside, and she didn't want to see it.

Suddenly all the horror of her nightmare was flooding back into her mind as if a dam had broken somewhere in her head.

I know what's in here, she thought, sickened and dizzy. But I don't know why someone sent it to me.

When enough of the plastic had been peeled

away, Aidan let out a soft exclamation. "The seascape?" he said, as Rachel backed away from the painting, her hands at her mouth. "Someone sent you the seascape? What for?"

"I don't know," she whispered.

They were silent for a moment, staring at the blues and the greens and the storm-tossed water. "Did you ever find out who painted it?" Aidan asked.

Silently, Rachel shook her head.

"Maybe he signed it before he wrapped it," Aidan suggested. "Check and see."

Rachel hesitated, biting her lower lip. Then she took a deep breath, let it out, and went back to the painting to strip away the last of the white covering.

A set of initials had been painted in the bottom right-hand corner in thick black oil.

Initials.

Four initials.

M.Y.O.B.

Rachel sank back on her haunches, letting out a soft, deep breath. At Christmastime when she was growing up, her grandmother often came home with overflowing shopping bags. When Rachel asked, "What's in the bags, Gram?" the answer was always the same: a warm, but firm, "M.Y.O.B., young lady. If you're a good girl, you'll find out soon enough."

M.Y.O.B.

Mind Your Own Business.

Rachel's head spun. The initials in the bottom right-hand corner of the seascape which had been delivered to her weren't an artist's signature.

They were a warning.

Chapter 6

"M.Y.O.B?" Aidan said. "That's his signature? Is that supposed to be a joke?"

"I don't think so," Rachel said, sinking to her knees in front of the painting. "I think it's a message for me. A warning. He doesn't want me telling people I see things in his work that others don't see. He wants me to keep quiet about it."

"You're getting all of that out of four initials?" Aidan's voice was skeptical. He dropped to his knees, too, his eyes on the painting.

Suddenly Rachel noticed something else about the seascape. The drowning figure was gone. Although she peered at the painting intently, the pinkish blobs that had seemed to her to be a screaming mouth and a pair of flailing arms were no longer there.

"It's gone," she whispered. "There isn't anyone drowning in this painting now. It's just a seascape."

"It always was, Rachel," Aidan said. "There was never anyone drowning in that painting. That was just a product of your imagination. I know art is subject to interpretation, but if you'll excuse the bad pun, you sort of went overboard on this one."

Because she couldn't deny what was sitting right in front of her eyes, Rachel would have agreed with him then, except for one thing. If she never had seen something sinister in the work of art, something that no one else had seen, why had the painting been delivered to her? And why were the letters M.Y.O.B. painted onto the canvas?

"If you paint something in oil and then change your mind about it," she asked, looking up at Aidan, "can't you just paint it out? Cover it up with another color?"

He nodded and got to his feet. "Sure. But that's not what happened here, Rachel. The painting looks exactly the way it always did."

"Then why," she asked, standing up and facing him, "was this sent to me?"

"Maybe the artist saw you admiring it at the exhibit," he said matter-of-factly. "Since no one else seemed to like it, he very generously decided you should have it. Don't you remember that old saying about not looking a gift horse in the mouth? You *do* like it, don't you? Just hang it somewhere and appreciate it. That's what art is for."

"But the initials," Rachel protested, waving a hand toward the painting. "You really think that's just a joke? Telling me to mind my own business?"

"You don't know that's what it means. Maybe those are really the artist's initials. Or maybe they stand for something else. Here," Aidan strode over to the painting and hefted it, "let me help you hang it. Where do you want it?"

Rachel shook her head. "I'm not sure I want to hang it at all. This whole thing is just too weird. Slide it under my bed for now, okay?"

Still holding the painting, Aidan hesitated. "You sure that's what you want?"

"Yes. I'm sure. I'll think about it tomorrow."

Shrugging, he bent to slide the painting under Rachel's bed. When he straightened up, he said, "Seems kind of rude, hiding it like that. But it's yours now, so I guess you can do whatever you want with it." Then, in a totally different tone of voice, he added, "Party at Nightmare Hall tonight. Feel like going? I'm not an atrocious dancer."

Struggling to push the painting from her mind, Rachel forced a grin. "Have you been dancing since you were eight, too?"

He returned the grin. "Twelve, but never with my brothers. So, how about it?"

Nightmare Hall was actually Nightingale Hall, an off-campus dorm in an old house. Sitting at the very top of a wooded hill, the house was old and creepy, so shrouded by tall, black oaks that its faded red brick seemed charcoal in color. It had been nicknamed "Nightmare Hall" after a suspicious death in the house. The name had remained long after the mystery had been solved.

The gloomy old house didn't appeal to Rachel, but she couldn't turn down a night with Aidan. "Sure. Sounds like a good time."

"Great. I'll give Sam and Joseph, maybe Paloma, a call, see if they want to join us, if that's okay with you."

Oh, peachy. "Sure. That'd be fun." Especially having Samantha along to steal Aidan's attention. Maybe she wouldn't be able to go.

But Samantha and the others were with them later as they drove up. It was the gravel driveway leading up the hill to Nightingale Hall.

Rachel's spirits lifted. The house didn't look nearly as threatening up close as it did from the highway. It was alive with lights and music. Several people sat on the porch swing laughing, others wandered the grounds. It looked pretty much like any other Salem U. party.

Once inside, however, Rachel viewed the steep, winding staircase leading from the foyer up to the second and third floors with alarm. It would be so easy for someone to trip on those stairs and take a terrible, bone-breaking fall.

Just like the image in the still life.

No. She wasn't going to think that way. Not tonight. She was there to have fun. Now, if only Samantha would meet a guy and vaporize for the evening.

"Does Sam have a boyfriend?" Rachel asked Paloma in a whisper as they moved through the crowded foyer to a large library, cleared now of all furniture except the floor-to-ceiling bookshelves, the carpet rolled back for dancing. The music was so loud, Rachel was sure the others couldn't hear her question to Paloma.

"Who?"

"Sam? Does she date anyone?"

"Well, you probably won't believe this, but I don't think she dates a lot. Most guys are intimidated by her looks and her money. That spells power to them, and in a way, they're right. Sam's a control freak. You should see her room. Everything perfectly in its place." Paloma continued, "She may not be much of an artist, but she'd make a great gallery owner or museum director. Very efficient, and she loves being in charge. She's pretty much running the exhibit, single-handed, although we're all supposed to be helping."

Rachel was surprised. That wasn't how she'd seen Samantha at all. In Sam's case, apparently, looks really were deceiving.

"She knows her art," Paloma said admiringly. "She'd make a great teacher, but she's one of the ones who won't be happy unless she's actually painting. Too bad."

But Paloma didn't sound as if she was wasting any pity on Samantha. She slid into a chair and surveyed the crowded room. "I think what Aidan likes about Sam, in case you're interested, is her knowledge of art."

Rachel's expression was glum. In a million years, she'd never catch up to Sam in that area.

"Just remember, Rachel," Paloma said, "if what Aidan wanted was someone to talk art to, he already has that in Samantha. My guess is, that's not what he's looking for."

"Thanks, Paloma," Rachel said.

Halfway through the evening, they were joined at their table by the party's hosts, three of Samantha's friends, whom Rachel had just met: Jessica Vogt and Ian Banion, who had been dating for some time, and Milo Keith, a quiet, bearded poet with a dry wit. All three lived in the off-campus house, and they entertained the group with unnerving stories of some very frightening incidents that had taken place in the house in the past. Any other time, Rachel would have been intrigued, and pressed them for more details.

But now, she found the stories unsettling.

To escape, she asked Aidan to dance with her. He was every bit as good at dancing as he was at volleyball, Rachel was glad to discover.

Bibi arrived with Rudy Samms. She was wearing a flaming red dress and heels that made her at least four inches taller than Rudy. He looked as glum as ever, and Rachel wondered how anyone could possibly have a good time with such a surly date.

But when she saw them dancing together later, she was astonished to see Rudy throw his dark head back and laugh aloud at something Bibi had just said. So, the guy did have a sense of humor, after all. Amazing.

Still, when she passed them later in the foyer, he was once again wearing that same dark, closed expression. How did Bibi stand that?

Each time Rachel passed the steep, winding

staircase at Nightmare Hall, she viewed it apprehensively, remembering what she thought she had seen in the still life.

But as the evening came to a close, Rachel breathed a sigh of relief. She'd been in the house for hours, and not once had someone taken a terrible tumble down the staircase.

She probably had imagined the falling body in the still life. An optical illusion, that's all it had been.

The vigorous game of volleyball and hours of dancing had taken their toll on all but Aidan. "I'm not ready to call it a night," he complained as they left the house.

"You never are," Joseph said. "If I hadn't seen you out in the sun for myself this afternoon, I'd swear you were part vampire. I'm going to hit the sack, and since I'm driving, I guess you'll have to come with me. Unless you want to walk back to campus."

Aidan looked at Rachel inquiringly. "You up for a hike?"

It was a nice night, balmy, with a star-sprinkled, navy-blue sky overhead. Rachel was tired, but the idea of just the two of them walking along the street alone was tempting. "Sure. Why not?"

It wasn't that far to campus. Rachel found herself wishing that Nightmare Hall was much further away. They began talking about the future. "Art is such a competitive field," Aidan admitted as, holding hands, they darted across the street to campus. "Tough to make a living, but not impossible. The safest way is commercial art, like advertising." He grinned down at Rachel. "You think I'd fit in on Madison Avenue?"

"I think you'd fit in anywhere you wanted to," she said staunchly.

"Yeah?" He put an arm around her shoulders and gave her a quick hug. "Thanks. Paloma's going to make a beeline for New York when she graduates, and Sam probably will, too. Sam would love the power of New York. But I think Joseph and I are going to head for sunny California after graduation, see if Disney Studios could use a couple of smart-aleck animators. Do the Mickey Mouse thing. Are you a Mickey fan?"

"His ears are too big. But I've always had a thing for Tweety Bird."

"He's not Disney."

"Does that mean I can't like him anymore?"

Aidan laughed. "You can like anyone you want to. As long as I'm on the list somewhere."

When they reached her room, he asked her once more if she'd like him to hang the painting before he left.

"Aidan, it's almost two o'clock in the morning." She opened the door and peered inside. "Bibi's not home yet, but you still can't be pounding nails into the wall."

"Only *one* nail. But okay. Tomorrow, maybe."

Why was he being so insistent about that painting, Rachel wondered after he'd left.

Deciding that she would never be able to sleep with it under her bed, she slid it free and hauled it over to the double closet she shared with Bibi, pushing the painting inside, against the rear wall.

Then she closed the closet door and padded back to her bed.

She got into bed thinking that of all the Saturday nights she'd spent on campus since late August, this one definitely was up there in the top ten. The day had started out so poorly, and ended so well.

But as she put her head down on the pillow, prepared to burrow into it as she always did, her left ear landed on something small, cold, and hard.

Rachel lifted her head. She had taken off her earrings before she'd undressed. Couldn't be an earring.

She reached over and switched on the bedside table lamp.

There, on her pillow, was a tiny brass monkey, like a charm for a bracelet.

It wasn't hers. She had never seen it before.

Its miniature paws were covering its eyes.

Rachel picked it up. She sat on the edge of her bed and looked down at the small charm.

She knew the symbolism of the paws over the eyes. Three monkeys. One with its paws over its eyes. "See no evil." Another with its paws hiding its ears. "Hear no evil." And still another with its paws covering its mouth. "Speak no evil."

The one she held in her hand was the "See no evil" monkey.

How had it got into her room, onto her pillow?

What was it doing here? What did it mean?

Rachel shook her head as she thrust the monkey under her bed and reached over to turn off the light. You *know*, she told herself, sliding down beneath the covers, her eyes wide in the darkness. You *know* what it means. It means the same as "M.Y.O.B." It means, don't see what someone doesn't want you to see.

Rachel flopped over onto her stomach. She felt stiff and tense again, as if the relaxation of the party had never taken place.

If someone didn't want her to see certain things, why was he painting them into his art?

She couldn't help seeing what was there, could she?

What was she supposed to do now? *Pretend* she didn't see what she saw?

She was grateful now that she hadn't told anyone what she'd seen in the still life. True, they'd all seen her staring, and must have wondered. But she hadn't actually said anything.

Who had put the brass monkey on her pillow? What was going on?

Sleep was a long time coming, and when it did, it was a restless, fitful sleep.

Chapter 7

The house that had been ablaze with lights only a few hours earlier is dark now, a hulking, ominous shape looming up from behind the oaks towering over it. A deep, unnatural silence has fallen over the hill, and not a leaf stirs on the trees or the shrubbery flanking the front porch.

Inside, the same, dark silence permeates the three-story house. But this silence is anxious, tentative, as if the house itself is holding its breath, waiting for something to happen. Something bad . . .

The first sound to break the silence is the creak of a door opening somewhere on the first floor. Then footsteps going up the staircase, soft, whispering footsteps, like that of feet wearing socks or moccasins.

The footsteps belong to a tall figure in flowing

black. It tiptoes along the darkened hall as if it knows its way.

A hand reaches out, turns a knob, opens a door. The figure disappears inside the room.

The room faces the skinny, rusted fire escape running along the outside of the house from the ground to the attic on the third floor.

It is a warm and balmy night, so the window is wide open, although no breeze stirs the white lace curtains.

The figure in black moves toward the bed, where deep, even breathing sounds.

The hand reaches out again, this time to shake a sleeping shoulder and whisper harshly, "Get up! There's a fire! Hurry!"

The dreaded word, "Fire" awakens the unsuspecting resident of Nightingale Hall. "What?" he whispers, the way people do in the dark, "what's wrong?"

"No time," the voice whispers back, "no time to talk. There's a fire! You'll have to climb out the window to the fire escape. Hurry, hurry!"

A sleepy-eyed, dazed Milo Keith, tall and skinny and bearded, jumps from the bed, instinctively grabs a pair of jeans lying crumpled on the floor and yanks them on. He reaches desperately for a notebook of his latest poetry lying on the bed, but the hand stops him. "No time. Go! Hurry!"

Milo stumbles to the open window. With one last, reluctant look at his possessions, which he believes are about to be lost forever in a roaring blaze, he climbs over the sill onto the ancient fire escape. He sees no sign of flames, smells no smoke, but thinks maybe the fire has begun on the opposite side of the house.

Before beginning to descend the fire escape, he turns slightly to say, "There's no one else out here. Is everyone in the house awake? Are they safe? I can help . . ."

Two hands reach out of the open window and push, hard.

Caught off guard, an already dazed Milo loses his balance, and, too startled to cry out, topples backward. His skinny legs flailing wildly, he tumbles end over end down the unyielding metal stairs. He does cry out once, only once, as the back of his skull takes a particularly sharp and painful blow. Still he continues to fall, propelled by his own momemtum, until finally he comes to a rest halfway down the metal stairs.

No lights go on inside the house. After an exhausting party, the residents of Nightmare Hall are too lost in sleep to hear that single cry.

Milo lies stunned, his legs dangling over one of the metal rungs. He fights to cling to consciousness. Blood trickles from his head.

Above him, the figure cloaked in black makes a muted sound of satisfaction, whispers something, then turns and leaves the room, not rushing, not hurrying, walking calmly.

Outside, the figure turns only once to look up at the fire escape at the side of the old, gloomy house. The hooded head nods at the sight of two legs dangling over the edge of a stair halfway down. The legs hang limply, lifelessly now, evidence that the victim has lost his valiant struggle to remain conscious.

Then, whistling softly, the black figure, just one more dark shadow among the gnarled old oaks, moves on down the driveway and up the street toward campus.

Chapter 8

Rachel jolted awake as if she'd been prodded with a hot wire. Her eyes flew open to bright daylight, telling her she must have had the nightmare during the last few moments of sleep.

She remembered every second of it. Every awful second.

Milo . . . Milo Keith, the skinny poet she'd met the night before at Nightmare Hall, had been in her nightmare. Rachel sat up in bed, scooting backward until she was huddled in a corner. Was Milo really lying on that fire escape, his head bloody, his legs still dangling over one rusted rung?

Or had someone discovered him by now?

Or . . . Rachel clenched and unclenched her fists . . . or had it never happened? Maybe this time it *was* just a nightmare. Maybe Milo was sound asleep in his own bed, unscathed.

She had to know for sure.

Leaning foward, she grabbed the campus telephone book from her bedside table and, a moment later, dialed Nightingale Hall's number. Bibi heard the pushbuttons clicking and groaned a complaint, but didn't fully awaken.

A woman's voice answered. "Mrs. Coates here," she said briskly. "Who's calling, please?"

Rachel didn't give her name. "Could I please speak to Milo Keith?"

"Oh, my dear," the woman said in a quieter voice, "that would be impossible. Milo has had a dreadful accident. He's been taken to the hospital in Twin Falls. I was just on my way there. If you'll give me your name, I'll be happy to tell him you called." She paused, and then added, "If he's conscious when I get there. He wasn't when the ambulance took him away. Took a terrible blow to the head . . ."

Rachel hung up. She sank back against the pillow, fighting nausea. It *had* happened. While Mrs. Coates hadn't actually said that Milo's "accident" had taken place on the fire escape, Rachel knew that it had. He had tumbled down those rusty metal stairs just like the figure in the still life.

No, no, no! Again, what she'd seen in a painting had come to life in a dream. And again, the terrible vision had become reality.

How was that possible?

Rachel's skin felt fiery, as if someone were holding a torch to it.

Would the still life arrive at her door, wrapped in white plastic, as the seascape had?

She buried her face in her pillow.

"What's the matter?" Bibi asked when she awoke a few minutes later and saw Rachel crumpled in a ball on her bed. "Are you sick? Too much partying?"

Rachel rolled over and sat up again.

"Rachel, what is *wrong* with you? You look like one of those masks Aidan's always making out of plaster. The ones at the exhibit. All white and pasty, like unbaked bread dough."

"Milo Keith fell down the fire escape at Nightmare Hall last night," Rachel said dully. "He's in the hospital."

Bibi's mouth made a round O of horror. "The fire escape? They had a fire at Nightmare Hall after the party?"

Rachel shook her head. "No. No fire. He just . . . he just fell. During the night." She couldn't tell Bibi that Milo hadn't fallen, that he'd been pushed, because then she'd have to mention the dream. Which Bibi would react to with scorn.

"How do you know?"

"I just called there. The housemother told me."

Bibi tilted her head, curiosity on her face. "If there wasn't a fire, what was Milo doing out on the fire escape in the middle of the night? And why were you calling Nightmare Hall at nine o'clock on a Sunday morning in the first place? Did you leave something there last night?"

Rachel didn't even hesitate. Bibi had just given her the perfect excuse for the phone call. "An earring. One of the garnet ones. It must have fallen off when I was dancing. And I don't know what Milo was doing out there during the night," she lied. "But I think he's seriously hurt. A head injury, Mrs. Coates said." She needed desperately to confide in someone about last night's horrible dream. But if she *did* decide to tell someone, it wouldn't be Bibi.

"Well," Bibi said, sliding out of bed, "I don't know Milo very well, but he seemed like an okay guy. I just can't figure why he would be out on that old fire escape in the middle of the night." Shaking her head at Milo's apparent foolishness, Bibi went off to take her shower.

I have to see the still life again, Rachel thought. Before the artist takes it away, as he did the seascape. Before he changes it. She had to see the staircase image again before the painting was doctored up and delivered to her as a "gift."

She jumped from the bed and darted to the closet. Slipping into a pair of jeans and a bright green T-shirt, she pushed her feet into sandals, ran a brush through her hair, grabbed her purse, and hurried from the room.

She raced across the relatively deserted campus, not even bothering to say hello to the few people she saw.

When she reached the art building, out of breath, and praying the still life would not be gone from the wall behind the pedestal, Rachel yanked the heavy wooden door open.

It was dim and cool inside, but not empty. Rudy Samms, armed with a duster and a yellow can of furniture polish, was working at a huge desk in the middle of the lobby.

"What are you doing here?" he called as she made a dash for the corner where the still life had been hanging.

She ignored him, focusing her eyes on the wall just ahead of her. When she was close enough, she breathed a sigh of relief. The painting was still there, in the same spot. It looked as if it hadn't been touched.

She'd arrived in time.

No, not quite. Because when she looked more closely at the painting, she realized with a sudden surge of fury that it had indeed been touched. Touched *up*, she corrected mentally.

The stairs and the flailing legs were gone. It was as if they'd never been there. The entire vase was now thickly layered with nothing but dove-gray swirls and brushstrokes.

She whirled and hurried over to Rudy. She knew he'd been watching her, but now he was pretending to concentrate industriously on his dusting. "Who's been in here this morning?" Rachel demanded.

"No one. Just me." He looked up lazily. "Why?"

"Are you sure? What time did you get here?'

"Seven. I'm always in early. No one gets here before me. Of course," he aimed a sly glance at her, "someone could have come into the lobby while I was upstairs, cleaning up the studios." He shook his head. "Have to be awfully careful up there, not to damage any of the precious 'works of art,' " he added sarcastically.

"You think someone came in while you were upstairs?" Rachel pressed sharply.

"I didn't say that. I said, someone *might* have. I can't be in two places at the same time, now can I? So," he shrugged as if to dismiss the matter, "who knows? Why? Something wrong?"

She wasn't going to learn anything from him. Rachel turned away. She had planned to take the painting with her when she left, take it to the police and show them the stairs and the falling legs hidden within the work. But there was no point now. All they would see was a vase filled with blue and lavender and mauve flowers.

She turned back to Rudy. "How do you get upstairs?"

He shot her a contemptuous look. "How do you think, Rachel? You either walk up the stairs or take the elevator, the same way you would in any other building on campus."

"I meant," she said coldly, "where is the staircase?"

He waved a hand toward the rear of the lobby.

"Are the rooms up there open? Unlocked, I mean?"

He nodded.

"I promised Aidan I'd come and take a look at his masks," she said. "That's why I'm here."

"Then why were you looking at that still life?"

And why are you so suspicious? she almost said. But she knew she needed him, so she said instead, "Aidan has a couple of masks on that wall, too, Rudy. Listen, I need a favor."

"What kind of favor? I'm busy."

Rachel said pleasantly, "If anyone comes in

and goes anywhere near that still life in the corner, would you come up and get me? I'll be in one of the art studios."

"I have work to do," he objected. "I can't be watching the door."

"Bibi would really be happy if you'd do her roommate this one favor," Rachel said, hating herself for using Bibi. But desperate times called for desperate measures. Rudy was all she had, and if she had to blackmail him into helping her out, so be it. "Rudy, there's no way you won't notice one lone person walking into the lobby. All I want you to do is come and get me. Use the elevator. It'll only take a second."

"Oh, all right. But I'm going to be done in here in a few minutes."

"I'll hurry."

And she did. She went from one studio to another, as vague about what she was looking for as she had been at the waterfall. But she couldn't bear to leave the art building without at least looking around. He had *been* here sometime during the night, slathering fresh oils on the still life. Maybe he'd left some sign, some clue . . .

The studios all smelled of paint and paint thinner. Rachel knew where she'd found the studio where Aidan worked because half a dozen of his masks lay on cloths on a table. There was a faint, mildewy smell of plaster.

Rachel was drawn to the masks. They were lying on a long, narrow table directly beneath a wall of short, wide windows. She recognized only one of the faces. Samantha's. There was no mistaking the perfect oval, the high cheekbones, the deep-set eyes, the confident set of the mouth.

Samantha had been braver than Rachel.

She wanted to pick up the mask and check the back for Aidan's initials, part of her hoping that someone else had taken the time and energy to create a mask of Samantha's face, not Aidan. But she was terrified that she'd drop it and it would smash into a thousand tiny pieces scattered all across the floor. Besides, she knew it was his.

She turned away from the table and glanced around the room. Did you really expect to find a black-hooded cloak hanging on a hook for everyone to see, perhaps with a bloody baseball bat hanging from its pocket? a voice in her head asked sarcastically.

She wandered over to a large supply closet, its door standing wide open, on the opposite side of the room. It was dark inside, but Rachel could make out a long, narrow space lined on both sides with floor-to-ceiling shelves and cubbyholes. Rachel stepped cautiously over the threshold. Boxes and cartons and plastic cases of art supplies spilled over the edges of the shelves, stretched empty canvases were stacked on the floor, metal cans of paint thinner sat just inside the door, and long-sleeved smocks had been discarded on the floor at the far end of the closet, forming a multicolored, paint-daubed mound.

Rachel walked back to the mound. When she noticed the name SAMANTHA WIDDOES written neatly in black ink on the inside of a collar, she bent to pick through the pile, searching for Aidan's smock.

There . . . AIDAN MCKAY, scrawled sloppily. Artist or not, his penmanship stank.

Rachel pulled the wrinkled, paint-stained smock from the pile and slipped her arms into the sleeves. She pulled it closed in front, trying to feel as Aidan must feel when he put it on and went to work. But she only felt silly. It was way too big for her.

The smell in the closet was giving her a headache.

She was about to remove the smock when she noticed the colors patchworked across the front. She wasn't surprised by the dried paint itself. She had known that was there, had expected it when she first picked up the smock.

But the colors caught her eye. Or, more precisely, the exact shades of color. Three egg-shaped blotches of bright green. Not the ordinary green of grass or trees, not the green of an avocado or of a turtle shell, but the vivid, startling green that she had only seen in one other place. The seascape. She had seen this exact, unusually vivid shade of green in the seascape.

And there, on the other side of the smock, half a dozen smaller splotches of a blue almost as brilliant as Aidan's eyes. The very same shade of blue that had pulled her to the seascape in the first place.

Below that, on the pocket, a round, uneven circle of the color that Samantha had called "mauve" in the still life. Next to it a slash of lavender and underneath that a blob of cornflower blue. All of the colors found in the still life.

Still wearing Aidan's smock, Rachel bent down to finger quickly through the rest of the mound, scrutinizing each of the remaining smocks for paint stains the same shades as those on the smock she was wearing.

No other smock bore those same telltale shades. Only Aidan's.

Rachel stood up, hugging the smock around her. Aidan hadn't painted those two paintings.

He *hadn't*. He would have said, if he'd painted them.

Well, no, Rachel, the voice in her head said, I don't believe he would have. Because whoever painted those particular works of art is up to no good, right? Isn't that why you're here? Because you believe that whoever painted those paintings also pushed Ted Leonides into the river and Milo Keith down the fire escape? Just like in your nightmares? So how likely is it that the artist of those two works would admit to having painted them? Use your head.

Rachel looked down at the splotches on the front of the smock. Aidan? No, he couldn't have painted those pictures. He didn't even *like* them. At least . . . he'd *said* he didn't like them. And had sounded like he meant it.

Her purse, which she'd deposited on the floor of the storage closet when she tried on the smock, was a large, roomy brown shoulder bag. Rachel removed the smock, rolled it up into as small a ball as possible and thrust it into the purse. She had no idea what she was going to do with it, but she knew she couldn't leave it there. It told her something, although she wasn't sure exactly what.

When Aidan noticed it was missing, he'd have no reason to connect the disappearance to her.

Rachel slung the purse over her shoulder and turned to walk back to the door of the closet.

She was almost there when she noticed a stack of canvases, piled on top of each other, on a high shelf just ahead of her. If they were signed, she might get some idea of each person's particular style, even with her limited art knowledge. Maybe she could figure out for herself who had painted the seascape and the still life.

But the shelf was too far up for her to reach.

Rachel glanced around. There was no ladder. How did they get stuff down from that shelf? Maybe there was a ladder somewhere else. But she didn't want to waste time looking.

Instead, she pulled half a dozen unopened cardboard boxes off the shelves and piled them on top of one another, creating her own "ladder." Dropping her purse on the floor and using a lower shelf as a stepping stool, she climbed onto the box pyramid, stood up, and grasping the edge of the top shelf with one hand, reached upward with the other arm to pull a canvas forward.

The top canvas was a charcoal sketch of Butler Hall, the administration building. She turned it over, the boxes teetering precariously beneath her. The initials on the back were S. W. Samantha. The drawing bore no resemblance to either of the oil paintings.

Rachel slid it back into place and was about to pull the second canvas toward her when she heard a noise at the door and then a scuffling sound below her.

Before she could look down, a voice whispered harshly, "Gotcha!" a forceful blow hit the middle cardboard box, and Rachel's ladder collapsed beneath her.

She had her right hand on a canvas as her tower of boxes gave way; her left hand clutched one of the shelves. Crying out in surprise and fear, she dangled, legs waving frantically, for just a second or two, struggling to maintain her hold on the shelf.

She dropped the canvas and would have grasped the shelf with her right hand, too, but it was too late. The fingers on her left hand were already sliding off the shelf. With a horrified gasp, Rachel began falling to the hard tile floor below.

Just before she hit the floor, she was vaguely aware of a door closing. The closet disappeared into darkness, followed by the sound of a key turning in a lock.

Then her head smacked into the tile. Rachel cried out in pain. Her eyes shut, and she disappeared into a deeper darkness of her own.

Chapter 9

The first thing Rachel was conscious of as she came to was a sharp, unrelenting pain at the back of her skull. When she put a hand back there and withdrew it, it came away warm and sticky.

She was bleeding.

It was so dark. Why was it so dark? Dazed and dizzy, Rachel felt a moment of terror, wondering if the blow to the back of her head had rendered her blind.

Then she remembered where she was, and how the light had gone off just before she fell. She was in the storage closet in an art studio on the tenth floor. And she was locked in.

Fighting nausea and confusion, she struggled upright. The room whirled like a carousel. She leaned against the shelves for support and closed her eyes.

When she opened them again, nothing had changed. She was still sitting on the cold, tile floor of the pitch-black closet.

The first thing to do, she thought weakly, is get some light in here. All she had to do was stand up, feel her way to the door, and flip the switch. Such a small thing, such an easy task, no problem.

But by the time she'd accomplished it, her nausea had increased tenfold and her vision was blurred. Her legs were so weak, she could hardly stand. She had to keep one hand on the shelving unit to hold herself upright.

Still, having the light on helped.

Rachel rattled the doorknob. Definitely locked.

Rachel leaned against the door, trying to gather her thoughts and figure out what to do. First, it wasn't as if she was in a deserted building with no one to help her. Rudy was around somewhere, and besides, this was the last day of the art exhibit. People would be coming to the building to see the paintings and the masks and sculptures before they were gone for good.

If she yelled and screamed, someone would hear her. Someone would come and let her out.

Okay, okay, don't panic, stay calm, she warned, keeping her breathing steady. This building is *not* empty. All you have to do is scream, at the top of your lungs. Someone will hear you.

Screaming wasn't easy, however, not when she was so sick and weak and dizzy. Getting enough air into her lungs to propel her voice through the thickness of the storage closet door and out into the hallway, maybe even all the way down to lower floors if there was no one else on this floor, was difficult. She had to try three times before she could summon up a sound above a whisper.

Gradually, she managed several loud cries for help. They echoed shrilly in the narrow space around her, each one stabbing at her already aching head like long, sharp needles.

When no one came in response to her cries, she tried again. Once, twice, three times — screams for help that made her throat raw and her chest ache.

Nothing.

There must be no one on the top floors but her.

And her screams would never carry all the way down to the lobby, where by now people were probably arriving for the exhibit.

Rachel took a deep breath, painful to her raw, throbbing throat. Okay. So no one had heard her. She couldn't just stand here and do nothing. There must be something . . .

Her purse. She had several plastic credit cards in her purse. Couldn't she use one to open the door? She'd seen it done on television. It had looked as if all the detective or policeman did was slip the piece of plastic between the door and the frame. Could it be that easy?

It was worth a try. The paint fumes in this place weren't helping her headache any. She wasn't going to wait around to be rescued.

Rachel glanced around for her shoulder bag. She had dropped it on the floor when she began her climb up the tower of boxes. It should be here somewhere.

But, although she went over every inch of the place, scanning the shelves, moving the toppled boxes this way and that, poking behind the cartons of art supplies and the cans of paint thinner, she found no purse.

The shoulder bag was gone.

And with it her credit cards.

And . . . Aidan's smock. Rachel flushed guiltily, remembering that she had confiscated the paint-stained smock, rolling it up into a ball and stuffing it inside her purse. But she'd had a good reason, hadn't she? And now it was gone, gone with the purse and the credit cards that might have helped her out of this mess.

Her back against the door, she sank to the

floor, and put her head in her hands. All she wanted was out of this horrible, smelly place. Was that so much to ask? Checking, she discovered that her head was still bleeding, and wondered how much blood you could lose before you sank into unconsciousness. If she fainted, and no one checked the closet, she might not be discovered until the following morning when the art students arrived and came for their smocks or supplies.

The thought of spending the entire day and, worse, a whole night, in the narrow, smelly closet was more than Rachel could bear. She pulled herself to her feet again, leaning against the door for support. There had to be a way out of here. Another door, a window?

And then she remembered the dumbwaiter. Used, Aidan had said, to tote art supplies to the upper floors from the lobby.

Where was that dumbwaiter? Where on the tenth floor did it stop?

Wouldn't a dumbwaiter in the art building logically unload into the supply closets of the studios? Wouldn't that make the most sense?

Leaving the door, Rachel unsteadily walked the length of the closet, glancing on both sides of her, looking for a little door to the dumbwaiter.

The walls were covered end to end with

shelving and those shelves were crammed full of supplies. If there was a small door behind there somewhere, how would she ever find it? Take everything off the shelves? That would take years.

Aidan had said he used the dumbwaiter a lot. So it wouldn't be hidden. It would be where he could get to it easily to unload it.

Rachel felt defeat sweeping over her, dragging her down. Maybe the dumbwaiter didn't empty into this closet, after all. It could go to any one of a dozen other studios on the ninth and tenth floors.

Unwilling to give up hope, she got down on her hands and knees and crawled along the floor, tears gathering in her eyes. She had to keep swiping at them with the back of a hand to clear her vision, and her head seemed to be on fire.

Crawling laboriously, scrutinizing the space underneath the bottom shelf as she slowly moved along the floor, she had almost reached the rear wall, where she would have to give up hope entirely, when she saw the stack of canvases leaning unevenly against the back wall in a small, bare space beside the end of the shelving unit. The carelessness of the way they were perched, slightly tilted, gave Rachel the impression that someone had tossed them there in a hurry. Maybe . . . maybe they weren't usually there. Maybe they were usually on the top shelf, where she'd seen the other canvases. Maybe whoever had stashed them there hadn't even realized they were covering up something important. Like a small door in the wall . . .

In her eagerness, Rachel misjudged the distance between the end of the shelving unit and the wall, and as she lunged forward to push the canvases aside, she drove her forehead into the sharp metal edge of the second shelf. The blow sliced a gash two inches long, and blood flowed freely, running into her eyes and further blurring her vision.

Not even feeling the pain, Rachel muttered an oath, grabbed the first thing at hand, a paint-stained rag on the bottom shelf, to staunch the flow, and when it seemed to have eased, she reached out again to shove the canvases aside.

And there it was . . . a wooden door just like the one in the lobby, a small metal knob perched on one side.

Awash in relief and renewed hope, Rachel pulled the door open.

There were the ropes, the pulleys, and the little cupboardlike box, sitting empty now. It was small, but so was she.

She lay on her stomach, staring bleakly at

the open, waiting cupboard. You're crazy, she told herself. The blow to your head has scrambled your brains. You are ten floors above the lobby. You're feeling sick and dizzy and exhausted, and you expect to haul yourself all the way down ten stories by pulling on those ropes? Not in a million years.

I wouldn't have to lower myself all the way down, she argued. The other studios might be open. I can just lower myself one floor, crawl out into another studio, and escape that way. I can do that. That's not so hard.

The wound on her forehead was still bleeding. She had to keep swiping at it with the rag to keep her eyes clear.

But what if the other studios are locked? she asked herself. Then what? You'll crawl out, you'll go to the door, you'll try the knob, and it won't budge. You'll still be shut in. Are you going to try that at every single floor?

There would be a telephone. She could go to the next floor, crawl out of the dumbwaiter into the studio, and call for help. And wait.

And then Rachel remembered, with a jolt, just how all of this had happened. She remembered that someone unseen had darted into the closet, had knocked the boxes out from under her, had grabbed her purse and run, locking the door after him.

What if he was still around?

What if he was, at this very moment, standing on the other side of the storage closet door, listening and waiting? He'd hear the dumbwaiter moving slowly, painfully. He'd know what she was doing. He would turn and race downstairs, much faster than she could let out the ropes. He'd be on the next floor waiting for her when she crawled to what she thought was freedom.

Too risky.

It was the lobby or nothing. Even if he was down there, waiting, when she arrived . . . *if* she made it . . . he wouldn't dare reveal himself with all those people around. She'd be safe.

Ten floors . . . she was so dizzy . . . it seemed impossible.

But she had no choice.

Keeping the rag with her to wipe her forehead, Rachel crawled forward, into the dumbwaiter. It lurched crazily when she entered. Her heart stopped as she grabbed for, and clutched, both ropes. She imagined the small, wooden cupboard free-falling under her weight, hurtling downward like an elevator with a broken cable, smashing into a thousand pieces when it hit the ground ten stories below.

But when she grabbed hold of the ropes, the dumbwaiter steadied itself. It slid downward again as she settled her weight inside, but when she pulled on the ropes with all of her strength, it stopped descending, swinging slightly.

Rachel pulled herself into as small a ball as possible, her head bent, her legs folded into her chest.

Then, taking only tiny little gasping breaths, she tested the two ropes to see which one would lower her. When she pulled on one, the wooden cage tilted slightly upward, telling her it was the other rope she needed to grasp.

Clutching it with both hands, she let it out no more than half an inch at a time. Had she been trying to haul her own weight upward, the task would have been too much for her. But gravity was on her side, and as she cautiously let the pulley rope out, the cage began, very slowly and unevenly, to descend, swinging very slightly from side to side, banging gently against the sides of the narrow shaft.

It took a thousand years for Rachel's precarious descent. Every nerve in her body was screaming with tension, and her fingers, palms, and arms throbbed in agony from the strain of her death-grip on the thick, rough rope. Four different times, her fingers jerked in a reflex action against the relentless tension, and four different times the dumbwaiter lurched sickeningly. Each time, Rachel gasped and tightened her grip again, nearly passing out from sheer terror.

The cupboard lurched and swung and banged against the sides, but it continued to lower itself. Because Rachel had to keep both hands on the rope, she was unable to swipe at the cut on her forehead with the rag, and as she continued her agonizing descent, blood from the wound began to pour anew, running down into her eyes and over her cheeks, onto her chin. But it didn't matter. There was nothing to see. There was no light in the shaft, nothing but pure darkness. Anyway, she thought, giddy with near-hysteria, it's not as if I need to see where I'm going. There isn't any other traffic in here.

The laugh that escaped her then quickly became a sob, and she had to bite down hard on her lower lip, bloody from her forehead wound, to keep more sobs from escaping.

At last there was a soft but definite bump as the dumbwaiter hit the bottom of the shaft.

She was on the ground floor. Safely. In one piece. The dumbwaiter hadn't fallen and crashed. It was now sitting solidly and securely on the ground.

Rachel sagged against the rear wall of her little cubbyhole. A sound came out of her mouth, half a gasp of relief, half a moan of exhaustion and pain.

When her breathing had steadied a little, she leaned forward and, with great difficulty, pushed open the small door facing her, without knowing or caring where it led. She was safe. It didn't matter where she was. She swiped at her forehead with the rag, and crawled out of the dumbwaiter.

All conversation in the lobby of the art building came to an abrupt halt. A crowd of horrified spectators watched as out of the small doorway emerged a figure with a blood and tearstained face, a nasty gouge across her forehead, and bloody palms.

Chapter 10

Because the cut on her forehead wasn't as deep as it had seemed, when the physician at the infirmary had ruled out broken bones from her fall and concussion from the blow to the back of her skull, Rachel was discharged, bruised and aching, a tube of cream in her hands for her raw palms.

Rachel's head ached. Her shoulders were throbbing and her hands hurt. She had already explained several times, to a wide assortment of teachers, security personnel, and friends, exactly what had happened. Without exception, they had all stared at her as if she had suddenly sprung antennae. She couldn't be sure that anyone believed her, although they had clucked and said, "Isn't that awful? Why, that's just terrible."

Rachel realized that the sight of her crawling out of the dumbwaiter must have been a terrible shock to all of those people gathered in the lobby viewing the artwork. If it hadn't been for Paloma and Samantha, she would still be sitting on a chair in the art building telling her story over and over again, trying to get someone in authority to comprehend it. The two girls had practically kidnapped her, insisting that she go to the infirmary before, as Sam put it, "she bleeds to death."

An exaggeration, but it got Rachel away from all those staring, disbelieving eyes.

Although Paloma and Samantha had been sympathetic, repeatedly asking her if she was okay, there were questions in their eyes, too. And Aidan, Joseph, even Rudy had done nothing but ask logical, annoying questions about what she was doing on the tenth floor, how she'd become locked in the closet, why she had risked the treacherous descent in the dumbwaiter, which wasn't meant for people at all.

As if anything that had happened to her lately could be explained away logically.

Having someone, anyone, understand what she'd gone through would have eased the pain just a little. They were all very, very sorry, *but . . .*

And when Rudy went back upstairs to check, the storage closet door was unlocked, and open.

When she said, "But my purse is still missing, isn't it?" someone, she wasn't sure who, suggested that she'd lost it down the dumb-waiter shaft when she crawled in.

The security guard took down what little information she could give him, but she could tell he was only doing it because it was his job. The look on his face told her he thought it was probably a crazy bid for attention, or maybe a sorority prank.

"I still don't get it," Aidan said as he walked her back to Lester. Everyone else had already returned to the art building, once they knew that Rachel was going to be okay. "You were standing on a pile of boxes? And someone kicked the pile out from under you?"

When she didn't answer, Aidan went on, "And what were you doing in the studio in the first place? You never did say."

No, and she wasn't about to now. What difference would it make? He'd asked her that question at least four times, and she still didn't know how to answer it. If she said she had been looking for some tiny piece of information — *anything* — about the artist who had painted the seascape and the still life, he'd give her that look again, the one that told her to leave it alone.

So, ignoring his questions, she asked one of her own. "Did anybody find my purse? I need it. It has my student I.D. in it, my credit cards, my bankcard, money. I'll be lost without it."

Aidan looked annoyed. "Oh, I get it. You're not going to tell me what you were doing in the studio, are you? That must mean you didn't have a good reason for being there. If you did, you'd tell me."

Rachel was annoyed, too. And tired and sick and scared. "You know, Aidan, you have this irritating way of focusing on *details* instead of seeing the whole picture." Shouldn't he be more worried about her safety than *why* she had been in the studio? "Maybe that makes you a better artist, but it doesn't make you such a great friend."

He stopped walking, an angry flush on his face. They were just a few feet from Lester. "Friend? Is that all I am? A friend?"

Rachel looked him square in the face. He still hadn't asked if she was okay. "I'm not even sure you're that, Aidan. Thanks for walking me back." And she turned and moved her stiff, aching body into the building, leaving him standing there with his mouth open.

She went straight to her room, ignoring the shocked expression on Bibi's face when Rachel walked in with a gash on her forehead and the front of her gray sweatshirt soaked with bloodstains. She went into the bathroom and shut the door, plunked herself down on the cold tile floor and burst into tears.

It felt good, letting them loose after holding them back for so long, and she would have cried for a long time, but Bibi wouldn't stop pounding on the door and shouting Rachel's name.

Rachel got up and let her in. Then, at Bibi's insistence, she poured out the whole, crazy story.

To her surprise, Bibi didn't give her *that* look. The gash on Rachel's forehead seemed to be enough proof for Bibi that all of it really had happened. When she had been assured that no, there were no broken bones and yes, Rachel was okay, she said, "Does Aidan know what happened?"

Rachel nodded reluctantly. She was beginning to regret what she'd said to Aidan. To take her mind off it, she said, "Bibi, Rudy was there, in the lobby, when I went upstairs. He was the only person who knew where I was. And he wasn't very nice when I asked him to keep an eye out in the lobby for someone looking at the still life. Later, when he went back upstairs after I fell out of the dumbwaiter, he said the storage closet door was unlocked. But it *wasn't*, Bibi! Either the person who locked me in there went back up later and unlocked it, or Rudy was lying."

Bibi sat back on her heels. "Lying? Why would Rudy lie?"

Rachel flushed. She should have known better. If she had to tell someone she didn't trust Rudy, that person shouldn't have been Bibi. Now, she'd alienated the one person who had seemed to believe her story.

"Forget it, Bibi." Rachel said quickly. "I'm just really, really tired. What time is it, anyway?"

Bibi glanced at her watch. "One o'clock."

Rachel pulled herself awkwardly to her feet. "I'm going to bed. Don't wake me up unless there's a fire or an earthquake . . . or someone delivers my purse."

"You lost your purse?"

Rachel nodded. "Well, I didn't really lose it. The person who knocked me down and locked the storage room door took it. No one believes that, or even that there *was* a person, but it's true."

As Bibi turned to leave, Rachel added, "Bibi, have you heard anything about what happened to Milo Keith?"

"I heard that he's still unconscious, that's all."

Thirty minutes later, Rachel was in bed and asleep.

Bibi sat on her own bed, watching Rachel

until she was positive her roommate was asleep. Then she got up quietly and left the room.

Someone is lying on a table in one of the studios. A girl, wearing jeans, her hair swept away from her face, her skin shiny with grease, plastic straws protruding from her nostrils. The plaster, liquid now like milk, is in a large glass pitcher on a smaller table opposite her right foot. A cardboard shelf has been placed under her head to catch any excess plaster as it's poured over her features.

She seems too vulnerable, so utterly trusting as she lies there, waiting for her face, all of it, her mouth, eyes, nose, every inch of her face, to be covered with the white liquid, which will thicken and harden into a complete life mask of the girl, who is very pretty, with smooth, clear skin, long, thick lashes, and a straight nose and full mouth.

A shadowy figure moves into view, tall and hulking, covered in flowing black.

Where are the other students, where is the professor? Why is the girl alone in the room with the figure in black?

He is talking soothingly to the girl, telling her it's okay, it's fine, no problem, won't take long, she'll love it, she'll love the great life mask he's making of her face, which has, he tells her, great bones, perfect for immortalizing in plaster.

When he approaches with the pitcher, the girl shrinks back, momentarily apprehensive.

But he reassures her, patting her shoulder with a black-gloved hand. The straws, he tells her, will allow her to breathe. "Don't worry. Relax. We want the mask to reflect your usual expression and not look grim and tense."

The girl breathes deeply in an effort to relax. She trusts the figure in black and doesn't seem to be questioning his odd attire as he moves closer, glass pitcher of milky liquid in hand.

"Ready?" he says, the pitcher poised. "You'll have a moment of panic when this stuff starts to cover your mouth, but remember the straws in your nose, okay? As long as they're in there, you can breathe just fine. Ready?"

She nods, and closes her eyes.

He begins pouring carefully. The milky white liquid spills out over her forehead, her closed eyes, across her cheeks, her nose, avoiding her nostrils from which the plastic straws protrude. When the plaster reaches her mouth, covering her lips, her legs jerk instinctively, and he cautions her gently to lie still. "Remember to breathe through your nose," he says, and she is quiet again.

He continues to pour until all of the girl's face except for her nostrils is covered with a thick layer of white.

He lifts the pitcher.

Lowers it again.

Then he bends close to her face. He is smiling beneath the black hood. He puts his mouth next to her ear and whispers, "Surprise!" and in one swift, calculated movement, he rips the straws from her nose and pours again, filling both nostrils with the rapidly drying plaster.

The girl stiffens on the table. Her arms would have flown up then to flail at the air, but he has dropped the empty pitcher to the floor and is pinning her arms at her sides. Her legs are free and she kicks those, wildly, frantically as the plaster in her nose begins to harden. Her chest heaves in a desperate effort to suck in air, her body bucks and thrashes, but his weight pressing on her arms keeps her pinned to the table.

"Like a dying butterfly," he says, almost sounding sad.

It only takes a few minutes.

When it's over, he bends, picks up the pitcher, walks to a nearby sink and rinses the glass container thoroughly. He dries it, takes it into the storage closet and lodges it on a shelf. When he comes back out, he returns to the still, silent figure lying white-masked on the table.

When the time is right, he reaches down and pulls the mask free. It comes off without effort. The face beneath it is almost as white as the plastic, although the lips are blue.

"I guess I forgot to mention that we weren't making a life mask, after all," he says. "We were making a death mask."

Rachel woke up screaming.

Chapter 11

As the nightmare evaporated, and Rachel realized she'd been dreaming, her screams died. No one came running to her door, pounding on it to find out what was wrong. When she turned her head slightly, she realized why. Sunshine was streaming in through the window. It wasn't night, it was a beautiful afternoon . . . Sunday, she thought . . . and everyone was outside, doing fun things.

Why had she had that obscene nightmare?

Rachel lay in bed, as silent and motionless as the young woman in her dream. There had been no oil painting this time, no hidden image to warn her of the nightmare to come. It had slithered into her mind on its own. From where? She had been told that dreams were a product of the subconscious mind. But she couldn't bear to believe that her mind could harbor images as ugly as those in this latest nightmare.

It was one thing to think she was having nightmares brought on by the hidden images in the oil paintings. Those, at least, she could chalk up to the power of suggestion. Sometimes, she knew, an image that you hardly noticed the first time you saw it, could sink into your mind and park there. Later, it could pop up when you least expected it, even in dreams, because it was in your subconscious. That could have happened to her because of the oil paintings.

But dreaming something as horrible as this newest nightmare without ever having seen anything that suggested such an atrocious act, was ten thousand times worse.

Rachel sat up, leaning against the wall. Wait a minute. She *had* seen something to suggest that dream. The masks. The white plaster life masks made by Aidan and the others. The process had been explained to her, and she had found it frightening. "Not for the claustrophobic," Joseph had said, and she had shivered in distaste.

Surely that explained this latest dream of horror, the worst yet. She hadn't created it with her own mind, after all. The masks had suggested it.

Was she the only person on campus whose subconscious was so easily manipulated? Did anyone else suffer as she did when they closed their eyes at night, after viewing the works of art in the exhibit?

Today was the last day the paintings and masks and sculptures would be on display. She couldn't wait until they were gone.

Except, they wouldn't really be gone. Joseph had said that after the exhibit, the works would be on display in shops at the mall, the bank in town, and in various buildings around campus. Unless she stayed in her room forever, she couldn't escape the paintings and masks entirely.

But she wouldn't look at them. Whenever she came across one, she would lower her eyes and hurry past it without taking in one single detail. That way, she wouldn't be able to dream about it later.

Her head hurt. Her palms burned, and her shoulders felt like giant hands had been playing tug-of-war with them.

That poor girl . . . lying on the table, the straws sticking out of her nostrils until the black-robed figure whispered in her ear, "Surprise!" and yanked the straws free. Grotesque. The whole, insane dream had been grotesque.

But then, so had the entire episode in the

art studio's storage closet, and that hadn't been a dream at all. She couldn't blame anyone for not believing it, not even Aidan. She had tried so hard to explain, but everything she'd said had only sounded weirder than what came before it.

And the only proof she'd had was the gouge on her forehead, which she'd admitted had been her own doing, and the bloody lump on the back of her head, which she'd also had to admit she'd sustained when she fell. In fact, the only thing her attacker had actually done to her was kick the boxes free and close and lock the door. There was absolutely no way to prove someone had actually done either of those things.

Rachel sat up, nervously running a hand through her hair and then wincing as her fingers slid into the bump on the back of her head. Deciding that she was not going to spend the rest of her life hiding in her room, she got up, took a long, hot shower which did a lot to ease her aches and pains, and dressed in jeans and a red T-shirt. She was combing her damp, curly hair when Bibi returned, holding a brown paper bag close to her chest. She hesitated in the doorway, her eyes apprehensive.

Rachel knew immediately that she didn't want to know what Bibi was carrying. And it occurred to her then that she had gone, in just

a couple of days, from someone who had awak-
ened every morning looking forward to the
day, to someone who had begun dreading every
passing moment. The thought filled her with
rage. Why was this happening? And how could
it have happened so quickly?

She sank down on her bed, holding the hair-
brush in her hands, her eyes on Bibi. It had
taken her so long to get over her parents'
shocking deaths. Her grandmother had been
loving and kind and welcoming, but still, it had
taken a long, long time to stop being angry
and sad and shake that unbearable feeling of
abandonment.

But she'd done it. And after that long, long
time, she had finally begun to feel safe and
loved again. It hadn't been easy. She'd had to
fight hard for it. And now someone . . . she
had no idea who . . . someone was trying to
take that away from her.

Rachel's lips tightened, and her spine stiffened. She wasn't going to give them an easy
time of it. They weren't going to take away
from her what she'd struggled so long for without a battle. "What have you got there?" she
asked Bibi. "It's for me, isn't it? Let me see
it."

Slowly, reluctantly, Bibi approached, holding out the package to Rachel. "It was sitting on the floor outside our room when I came back," she said. "I looked inside, Rachel. I didn't know it was for you. There wasn't any name on the bag."

Rachel reached inside the folded bag and pulled out her brown shoulder bag. Confused, she looked up at Bibi. "But this is great, Bibi. Now I don't have to cancel my credit cards or apply for a new driver's license. This is terrific. Why didn't you want to give it to me?"

Bibi sat down on the floor at Rachel's feet. "Look at it, Rachel," she said quietly. "Look at the back flap."

Now it was Rachel's turn to hesitate. Bibi's voice told her too much. Bibi had seen something when she checked inside the brown paper bag that wasn't going to make her roommate happy. Rachel lifted her head to gaze out the short, wide window. The sun was shining so brightly, it made her eyes ache, and the sky was almost as brilliant a blue as Aidan's eyes. Such a beautiful day, why ruin it by seeing something that was going to make her miserable?

"Maybe I'll wait until later," she said, still gazing out the window. "Maybe I won't look at it just now."

"No," Bibi said firmly, "I don't think that's a good idea, Rachel. You'd better look at it now."

Rachel tore her eyes away from the window and looked down again at the purse. It looked so innocent, lying there in her lap, the brown leather shoulder bag she had hoped would show up. Now it had, but she wasn't rejoicing, was she?

"You're right," she said, remembering her resolve to fight against whatever was threatening her safety. "I'm being silly. It's probably nothing."

Bibi's expression said quite clearly that it wasn't "nothing." But Rachel turned the purse over, anyway.

Paper-clipped to the back flap of her purse was a page torn from a small desk calendar. Every day following Sunday had been slashed through with vivid red paint. Scrawled across the top of the page in the same shiny red were the words YOU WILL NEVER SEE AN-OTHER MONDAY.

Monday. Tomorrow. She was never going to see tomorrow? Or any other tomorrow?

Holding the defaced calendar page gingerly, Rachel looked up at Bibi. "Is there more inside?" she asked quietly, her voice strained.

Bibi's blonde ponytail flew as she shook her

head. "I didn't have the guts to look. I don't think you should, either, Rachel. That message on your purse is enough to take to campus security. Let's just take the purse and go to the security office and let *them* look inside, okay?"

Rachel's expression was grim. "No. It's my purse. I'll look."

"Rachel, you don't know what's *in* there. That's a *threat* on the flap. The purse could be booby-trapped or something."

Rachel uttered a short, harsh laugh. "Booby-trapped? You mean like with a bomb? I thought I was the one with the imagination. I'll bet there isn't anything at all inside. Someone is just trying to scare me." She laughed again, without humor. "Like I'm not already."

Bibi, her eyes wide, scooted backward on the floor until her back bumped into the desk chair. She sat on the floor, watching.

Rachel picked up the purse, pulled the zipper open, and peered inside. Then, frowning, she slid her fingers inside and when she withdrew them, she was holding a small, white plastic-wrapped package in her hands.

"Rachel, please don't open that," Bibi begged. "Please!"

"Oh, come on, Bibi," Rachel said lightly, dropping the purse on the floor to begin untying the twine around the white plastic, "you know what they say. Good things come in small packages, right?" But her fingers were shaking as she tugged at the twine.

They were so lost in the moment that when a knock came on the door, both jumped and cried out.

"Rachel, it's Aidan. You in there?"

"And Joseph and Paloma," Paloma's voice called. "We're here, too."

"And Sam," Samantha added, laughing.

Bibi sighed with relief and jumped up to let them in. "Now I don't have to be the only one witnessing the unveiling," she said over her shoulder as she opened the door. In a rush of words, she told the group what was going on. Her words tumbled out in a jumble that no one grasped.

They were still puzzled as they came inside and saw Rachel sitting on the bed unwrapping the package.

Bibi scooped up the purse and showed them the words scrawled in paint on the calendar page.

Paloma paled visibly, Joseph uttered a quiet oath, Aidan hurried over to Rachel's side and sat down on the bed beside her, and Samantha said sensibly, "Rachel, you should have just taken that package to security."

"I told her the same thing," Bibi said, sitting

down on her own bed, "but she wouldn't listen."

"I knew it was a painting," Rachel said as she peeled away the plastic to reveal a small, rectangular object. She held up the object, facing it toward them so they could all see it. "And that's exactly what it is."

It was indeed a painting. A small one, perhaps five inches across and seven inches high, but definitely a painting, done not in oil this time, but pastel water colors: pink and mauve and rose on a white background.

Everyone stared at the small work of art, but Rachel didn't need to. The minute she'd pulled the last of the plastic away, she had known what she would find. Her nightmare . . . this time, *after* the fact. And indeed, that was exactly what she saw in the painting, although she doubted that anyone else would see it in the muted haze of pink and rose and white.

At first glance, it appeared to be another still life, this one also of flowers. This time, the pink and rose flowers were in a field or a rambling garden.

But Rachel saw clearly, among the vague circles and swirls of pale pink and rose, the white table, the ghostly figure lying motionless on the table, the white death mask covering the young woman's face.

No one else would see it, of course. They

hadn't seen the drowning figure. They hadn't seen the figure tumbling down the flight of stairs. If those images had been cleverly hidden within the strokes of oil, this hidden image of the figure lying on the table among the pale watercolors was even more vague. Rachel thought that she wouldn't even have seen it herself if she hadn't already had the dream.

How could she have had the nightmare *before* she'd seen this painting?

"That calendar page is from the desk in the art building lobby," Joseph said. "See that little design at the top, the crisscrossed pen and paintbrush? But I don't get it," he added, furrowing thick, dark brows. "The words are scary, but the painting isn't."

"Look at it closely," Rachel said, knowing it was futile, but passing the small painting around, anyway. "Don't you see *anything* in that painting but flowers?" It was maddening, being so certain of what she was seeing and, at the same time, being incapable of making them see it, too.

They passed it from hand to hand, each of them studying the watercolor carefully, looking for some hint of what the message on the purse had threatened.

No one but her saw anything.

It doesn't matter, Rachel thought dispiritedly as she retrieved the painting from a bewildered Aidan. The hidden images weren't meant for any of them, anyway. They were meant for only one person. Me. And *I* see them.

The artist had accomplished what every artist wanted more than anything. He had achieved his goal in painting the watercolor. He had sent a message, and the message had been received.

The message was: Rachel Seaver, you are going to die.

Chapter 12

"That looks like something you'd do, Sam," Joseph said to Samantha, pointing at the watercolor in Rachel's trembling hands. "It's got your touch. All those dull, weak pastels. And it *is* a watercolor, your specialty."

"Who are you kidding, Joseph?" Samantha said, leaning over Rachel to study the small painting. "You've never paid enough attention to my work to have any idea where my real talent lies."

"What talent?" Joseph murmured.

Rachel hurt for Samantha, although Sam herself seemed unperturbed by Joseph's comment. She never even glanced at him. "Everyone's a critic," she said dryly, and then tapped a finger on the watercolor and said to Rachel, "It's just a painting, Rachel. It can't hurt you. But I don't blame you for being upset about the calendar. That's pretty creepy."

"And Joseph's right," Paloma said, "that page is from the calendar in the lobby of the art building."

"Which means," Aidan pointed out, "that any one of hundreds of people who viewed the exhibit could have helped himself to that page. No one would have noticed someone pocketing a calendar page."

Rachel wasn't listening. She was staring at the painting. Flowers . . . so many flowers . . . like at a funeral.

YOU WILL NEVER SEE ANOTHER MONDAY.

Who had stolen her purse? Kicked those boxes out from under her? Locked that closet door?

Rachel felt as if her brain was rapidly disintegrating. What was left of it remembered that she had put something in her purse before she'd climbed up on those boxes. What was it? What had she confiscated?

Oh. A smock. Aidan's smock. Because of . . . because of the paint stains, the colors.

She slid her hand into the purse again, fumbling around, even though she was certain now that she wouldn't find what she was seeking.

Because it wasn't there.

Aidan's smock was gone.

She glanced up at him, her heart denying what her brain was thinking. The truth was, Aidan could have painted this simple watercolor with one hand tied behind his back. And only Aidan would have any reason to remove that smock, with its telltale paint blobs, from her purse.

"What's the matter?" he asked when he noticed that she was staring at him. "Why do I all of a sudden feel like I have two heads?"

Rachel's silence gave her away.

Aidan's eyes narrowed. He said quietly, intensely, "You just put me on your list of suspects, didn't you? You think I sent you that calendar page? Why would you think that, Rachel?"

"I never said I thought that, Aidan." Then, boldly, "I mean, there isn't any reason why you *would*, is there?"

Aidan looked as if she'd slapped him.

"Rachel!" Paloma gasped, clearly shocked. "How could you suspect Aidan?"

Samantha, however, said nothing, which Rachel found interesting. If anyone were going to rush to Aidan's defense, she would have expected it to be Sam. They seemed to be such close friends. Maybe Sam knew something about Aidan that no one else did.

"I would just like to remind you," Aidan said

icily, "that while you were *supposedly* trapped in that supply closet, I was downstairs in the lobby making small talk about art with two professors and a teaching assistant. If you'd like to check with them, I'd be happy to give you their names."

But Rachel didn't feel like backing down. Hadn't she dreamed about someone being suffocated with a death mask? Aidan made those masks. Others did, too, but he was the best at it. Maybe that particular nightmare had been her subconscious, warning her not to trust him. And as far as Aidan's alibi went, he could have slipped away from the lobby conversation just long enough to take the elevator upstairs, grab her purse, and lock her in the closet. He could have been back downstairs before anyone even noticed he was missing.

Everyone was staring at her.

Rachel didn't want to think these things about Aidan. If she could be that wrong about someone she was attracted to, that made her too stupid to live. Also, she was *still* attracted to him, and already sorry that she'd hurt his feelings.

"Look," she said, laying the purse aside, "I'm sorry, Aidan. I didn't mean that. But you don't know what it was like, any of you. You don't even seem to believe that it all happened the way I said it did. Being trapped in that awful place, thinking I'd never get out, and then that horrible ride down in the dumbwaiter. I've never been so scared in my life. And now *this*," holding up the calendar page. "So don't expect me to act rationally, because I don't think I can, okay? I'm shaking inside."

"Well, I believe you," Bibi said, taking the watercolor and the calendar page from Rachel. "We need to take these to the security office. But for now, you need to go out and do something to take your mind off all this. I'll put these things in your top drawer."

"We have to take some stuff from the show to the mall," Sam said. "Rachel, come with us. You can't stay here alone."

"And I won't be here." Bibi picked up her own purse. "I promised Rudy I'd help him take a load of paintings to the mall."

Rachel didn't want to go to the mall. She didn't want to go anywhere. But if Bibi wasn't going to be here, neither was Rachel. The purse had been delivered to her room. Maybe the mystery artist was lurking outside in the hall at that very moment, chuckling gleefully over her imagined reaction to his "gift."

Bibi turned to the others, asking, "How about it? A trip to the mall will do Rachel good. Help her forget about all this stuff. You know what they say: When the going gets tough . . ."

"The tough go shopping," Sam finished, laughing. Just as quickly, she sobered. "This is more than tough going, what's happening to Rachel. This is very scary stuff. But," she went on more cheerfully, "it's probably just a joke, anyway, Rachel. Someone playing games."

Rachel didn't know if anyone else in the room believed that, but she certainly didn't. Not for a second.

But she got up and grabbed a jacket from the closet.

Aidan shrugged and nodded.

"We'll have to be back by six to clean up after the exhibit," Joseph reminded all of them. "But I guess a quick trip to the mall isn't such a bad idea. And if we take a few of the paintings now, we won't have so much to take later. I'll miss seeing new viewers *ooh* and *aah* over my work, but I've had so much of that already. I wouldn't want to get a swelled head."

"Too late," Samantha quipped. "Rachel, you ready?"

"Yes," Rachel said, pulling on her jacket and following the others out of her room.

Chapter 13

There were still spectators viewing the exhibit when Rachel and her friends arrived, but Paloma suggested they take the first group of jewelry she had had on display, and half a dozen paintings that the artists had replaced with new ones for the last and most important day of the showing.

Joseph drove to the mall. Samantha shared the front seat with him, a group of canvases at her feet, while Rachel found herself sandwiched into the backseat between Paloma and Aidan. Bibi had decided to stay behind to help Rudy begin the cleanup.

Paloma carried her jewelry in a white shoebox on her knees. "Mr. Stein at the jewelry store in the mall wants to see my best pieces," she said happily. "I figure, if those sell, and I start getting a name for myself, then I won't have any trouble selling the pieces that aren't quite as good."

"You don't *have* any pieces that aren't quite as good," Joseph said generously. "Everything I've ever seen of yours has been perfect. You've never once messed up, the way I did in my pathetic attempts at creating life masks."

"How unlike you, Joseph," Samantha said drily. "That is the first and only time I have ever heard you pay another artist a compliment."

"Well, if you'd paint something besides those watercolors that look like they were left out in the rain," Joseph replied, "I'd compliment you, too."

"They're *supposed* to look like they were left out in the rain," Samantha countered.

"Sam, you haven't really discovered the power of painting until you've worked in oils," Joseph insisted.

Rachel stopped listening. Being in the car with people who were talking casually about art seemed surreal to her. Her life had been threatened, and yet here they were, talking about Samantha's watercolors and Paloma's jewelry. How could they? Why weren't they all discussing how she might protect herself, how she might escape from this horrible nightmare that was holding her in its grip, how she might live to see Monday?

Maybe they thought she didn't want to talk about it. She certainly hadn't been all that talkative back in the room. But that had been because she hadn't been sure they'd take her seriously. They didn't seem to be grasping the truth. One person had died, another had been seriously injured and was still unconscious, and more important, someone had connected those events to *her*.

She had no idea why. She hadn't known Ted that well, or Milo, either. And no one knew she'd had the dreams.

How could she blame her friends for not grasping what was going on? They hadn't seen what she'd seen in the paintings, and they hadn't had the nightmares.

But what *did* they think was going on? Did they really believe that Ted's death and Milo's fall had been accidental, that her entrapment in the storage closet had been a fluke of some kind?

Joseph and Samantha were still discussing art when Aidan took a corner too fast. The shoebox on Paloma's lap slipped off her knees and slid to the floor, the lid flopping off as it landed. Jewelry spilled out across Paloma's black, high-button shoes.

Rachel bent to help pile the pieces back inside their container.

When she saw the bracelet, she thought at first that she was imagining it. She closed her eyes, shook her head to clear her vision, but when she opened her eyes again, the bracelet was still lying in the palm of her hand, and there was no mistaking its design.

It was a simple gold chain from which dangled half a dozen tiny brass monkeys.

Rachel looked at it more closely. Two of the monkeys had their tiny paws over their mouths. Two were covering their eyes, and two more were shielding their ears from sound. The first one was identical to the monkey she had found lying on her pillow.

"Paloma?" Rachel said softly. "Did you make this bracelet?"

Paloma, busy scooping jewelry off the floor of the car and back into its shoebox, glanced up to see which piece Rachel was asking her about. She nodded. "Yeah, I did. Like it?"

"The 'see-no-evil' bracelet?" Samantha asked from the front seat. She turned her head toward Rachel. "I have one. I liked Paloma's so much, I had her make one for me."

"I already have the monkeys made," Paloma said to Rachel. "I made a bunch of them at the same time. So putting a bracelet together for you wouldn't take any time at all. In fact, I keep them in that storage closet you were stuck in. If you'd snooped around at all, you'd have come across them."

The expression "stuck in" wasn't lost on Rachel. Paloma hadn't said "locked in" or "trapped in," she'd said "stuck in," as if the door had accidentally, innocently, jammed. As if being trapped there and having to make a dangerous escape by dumbwaiter could have happened to anyone, anytime.

But Rachel was too preoccupied with the shock of seeing the tiny brass monkeys to focus on Paloma's choice of expression. Unwilling to release the bracelet, Rachel stared down at it, still in the palm of her hand. Paloma and Samantha both owned bracelets like this one? "Have you made more bracelets like this one?"

"Sure." Paloma covered the shoebox. "Half a dozen or so. Why?"

In a way, Rachel was relieved. When she had first seen the bracelet, her instant reaction had been to suspect Paloma. But if Samantha and half a dozen other people on campus owned similar bracelets, any one of them could have put that monkey on Rachel's pillow as a warning.

And Paloma had said she kept more of the tiny monkeys in the storage closet. "Do you keep them locked in something?" Rachel asked. "Like a strong box, something with a key?"

Paloma reached up to adjust her black velvet choker. "Locked up? The monkeys? No. Why would I lock them up? They're just brass, Rachel. They're not all that valuable."

That meant that everyone in the art department had access to the charms. Great. The art department had a lot of people in it.

At the mall, while Paloma talked with the jewelry shop manager, Aidan dragged everyone else into a nearby shop called African Safari. It was filled with exotic clothing and accessories, live plants, books, and photographs. On the wall near the door hung a cluster of masks carved of dark wood, the reason for Aidan's enthusiasm.

The masks were unlike anything Aidan made. The wood was smooth and shiny, the features painted on in vivid colors. Some had hair, some heavy wooden earrings dangling from lobes.

Aidan stretched up his arm to lift two of the more exotic masks off the wall. Holding one up in front of his own face, he thrust the other toward Rachel. "Here, try it on for size. It'll give me some idea of the dimensions I'll need when I make your life mask."

At the words "life mask," Rachel went

deathly white and backed away from Aidan so fast, she stumbled and nearly fell over a display of baskets behind her on the floor.

"Rachel, what's wrong?" Samantha asked.

And Aidan, still extending the wooden mask, echoed, "Rachel? These things don't bite. Go ahead, try it on!"

Rachel shook her head. "I . . . I . . . let Sam try it on."

"I don't *want* Sam to try it on," Aidan said sharply from behind his own mask. "I want you to. Come on, be a sport."

But Rachel was still backing away, moving toward the door. "I don't feel very good," she said. "I need some air. I'll meet you outside by the front entrance."

"There's a terrace right around the corner," Joseph said.

But Rachel was already gone.

She ran blindly through the mall, not thinking about where she was going, just wanting to go *anywhere*, to get away from the endless horror she'd been facing the past few days.

Finally, she reached the big glass doors of the mall and hurried through them.

Off to one side, she spotted a bench and went to sit down and catch her breath. The bench was directly beneath the terrace Joseph had mentioned.

Above her, Rachel could see red flower blossoms peeking out from underneath the metal railing. It was probably very pretty up there, but she felt much safer down here, with all these people hurrying past.

Joseph had told them they were supposed to be back at the art building by six o'clock and she glanced at her wristwatch to check the time. Only four-thirty. Plenty of time.

Still, she hoped the others wouldn't spend all afternoon in the mall. She was safe enough out here, sitting on a bench watching shoppers pass by with their trophies, but it didn't strike her as a really fun way to spend a day.

Aidan was probably mad at her for refusing to try on the masks. Was that why he hadn't come with her?

Something moved above her, and Rachel glanced up.

What she saw was the huge pot of bright red blossoms.

It was no longer sitting under the metal railing.

With a stab of terror she realized that the heavy pot of flowers had fallen off the edge of the stone terrace above her and was descending, at an astonishingly rapid speed, straight for her.

Chapter 14

Rachel sat frozen on the stone bench, her head tilted, disbelieving eyes riveted on the heavy pot plunging down upon her. If a shopper emerging from the mall just then hadn't seen what was happening and screamed a shrill warning, the pot would have slammed into Rachel full force.

The scream yanked her back to awareness. She catapulted her body backward, as hard as she could, off the bench and onto the grass. She landed on her back, one foot not yet free of the stone bench. The huge, heavy, terra-cotta pot slammed into the bench, instantly exploding into chunks of clay and sprays of dirt and red blossoms. There were screams and shouts as razor-sharp pot shards imbedded themselves in a forearm carrying a shopping bag, a hand counting change for the bus, the neck of the woman who had screamed a warning to Rachel. A toddler screamed in rage as a clod of dark dirt splashed his face and eyes. Another small child recoiled in terror, hiding his face in his mother's coat, while a group of teenagers lounging far enough away to escape injury watched with barely concealed delight at this unexpected relief from their chronic boredom.

Pandemonium reigned under the mall canopy.

Rachel didn't move. She couldn't. Her left foot was pinned against the stone bench by a large chunk of pot, dirt and flowers. It hurt. She could see a thin stream of blood dripping from the bench. Her blood. But she knew she was lucky to be alive. If that woman hadn't screamed . . .

Rachel swallowed a belated scream of her own. Then, because there was absolutely nothing she could do to help anyone, she lay back down on the grass and waited, her eyes wide open, staring up at the cloudless blue sky overhead. It was a pretty day, picture-perfect. And it had almost been the last day of Rachel Seaver's short life.

She closed her eyes.

And opened them again when she heard Aidan's voice above her saying, "I knew you should have stayed with us! Are you okay?" And then, "Rachel, you're bleeding. Your foot . . ."

"I know," she said calmly, looking up at him. "The pot fell. I was sitting on that bench when it came crashing down from the terrace. Just a second ago, I was sitting on that very bench."

Although she spoke calmly, Aidan got the picture. As Samantha and Paloma arrived, breathless with shock, Aidan began scooping the mound of debris off Rachel's foot. When it was completely uncovered, he carefully wrapped his windbreaker around the injured foot, bleeding steadily from a deep cut just above the anklebone. Then he knelt by Rachel's side, awaiting the ambulance.

Security officers busied themselves helping the injured, consoling the frightened children, asking questions.

Rachel had turned her head toward the entrance. Even in her shock, she couldn't help being amused by the change in expression on shoppers' faces as they emerged from the mall. They came out laughing or chattering with friends, or they came out alone, lost in thought, but no matter what they were doing when they came through the glass doors, their faces transformed completely when the scene of havoc before them registered.

Paloma and Samantha had been laughing too when they came out of the mall, laughter that died an abrupt death when they saw the chaos. Rachel was surprised to see Bibi and Rudy Samms trailing along behind them. Samantha dropped her packages and rushed over to the grassy area.

"Where did Bibi and Rudy come from?" Rachel murmured. "I thought they were still at the art building."

Aidan shrugged. "Who knows? Everyone left African Safari right after you did. They all had other places they wanted to go, so we said we'd all meet out here. They must have run into Bibi and Rudy inside."

By now, Rachel was surrounded by a small crowd. And the buzz of conversation around her made it clear that everyone was assuming the pot had simply fallen off the terrace.

All by itself? Rachel thought, disgusted. A great big pot like that? Oh, right. Like it was dancing or doing calisthenics and missed a step and tumbled right over the edge? So careless of it.

And people thought *she* was imagining things.

How could anyone possibly think that huge, heavy pot had somehow, all by itself and accidentally, fallen from the terrace?

Someone had pushed it. She knew it, in her heart and in her head. And toppling something that heavy must have taken strong muscles and a ton of determination.

But she was told, a few minutes later by the mall security officers, that no one had been on the terrace before the pot fell.

"It didn't just fall," Rachel insisted as the ambulance arrived with a mournful wail of its siren. "It couldn't have. Someone pushed it." Hadn't she said the same thing about Milo? No one had believed her then, either.

Milo . . . he was the reason Rachel changed her mind about refusing to go to the hospital. She had hoped to be taken to the campus infirmary for a quick dressing of her ankle wound, and then straight to her room and to bed.

But . . . if she went to the hospital, as the ambulance attendants were insisting, maybe she could hunt Milo down and, if he was finally conscious, ask him about the fire escape incident. If Milo remembered being pushed, she'd have someone backing her up. That would certainly help, wouldn't it? Then when she took the calendar page to security, she could tell them to go talk to Milo and they'd know the danger was real. Very real.

To her surprise, Aidan made it clear that he

and the others didn't believe the incident had been accidental. And he said so, first to Rachel, then to the mall security personnel.

Listening to Aidan and the officer argue, Rachel found herself much more interested in how long Rudy Samms had been with Bibi. Was he with her when the pot had come crashing down? Because if he wasn't, he just might have been out on the terrace, giving the huge planter a wicked nudge.

She knew she found it easier to suspect Rudy because she didn't like him as much as she did the others. Maybe that was unfair, but she couldn't help it.

"She got this message," Aidan was saying to the security officer as Rachel was loaded onto a stretcher. "Threatening her. Saying she wouldn't live to see tomorrow. That's why we're pretty sure the pot didn't just fall all by itself. Has one ever fallen before?"

"Not since I came to work here."

"Enough said," Aidan said firmly. He told Rachel they'd meet her at the hospital.

"No, Aidan," she said quickly, "you don't have to." If they all came to the hospital and waited for her to be treated, she'd never get to track down Milo. They'd insist on whisking her off to her room and tucking her into bed, safe and sound. "I could be there a long time.

You know what emergency rooms are like. And I know you guys are supposed to be back at the art building by six. You go ahead. When they've fixed me up I'll call you there. Someone can come down and pick me up then, okay?"

Not long afterward, she came out of the emergency room with stitches and a thick bandage on her injured ankle.

All she had to do was locate Intensive Care, where they were keeping Milo, and hobble there to see if he was awake.

She found ICU easily enough, but once there, she hit a snag. Only immediate relatives were allowed to see the patients. How was she going to get in to see him?

There he was, right there behind a large glass window. She could see him clearly. He didn't look conscious. He didn't even look alive. Much of his head was swathed in a thick white bandage. Even from a distance, Rachel could see how badly he'd been injured. His face was swollen and purple, with traces of dried blood zigzagging his chin and cheekbones.

For a unit filled with critically ill patients, there didn't seem to be that many nurses. One behind the high white desk off to Rachel's right, another moving briskly in and out of the room where Milo lay, still another further down the hall, where there had to be other rooms. Rachel waited until the nurse at the desk had turned her back and the nurse in Milo's area left his room and disappeared down the hall. Certain the nurse wouldn't be gone long, Rachel made her move.

It was easy. She simply opened the door and went into the unit, where she moved quickly into Milo's room and hurried to his bedside. Sooner or later, someone would notice her, but by then, maybe she'd already have her answer.

"Milo?" she whispered when she was at his bedside. Both eyes, the area around them swollen and black and blue, were closed. She imagined his head bouncing down the iron fire escape steps, and winced. His face looked so awful, it was hard to believe he'd ever appear normal again. "Milo, are you awake? Can you hear me?"

His eyes remained closed, the lids bluish, but he turned his head toward her when she spoke.

"Milo, it's Rachel Seaver. Someone's going to come and drag me out of here any second now, so if you can hear me, please tell me why you fell down that fire escape, okay? I need to know. It's important, Milo. A matter of life and death."

Milo forced one eyelid open slightly. When he spoke, his voice was hoarse, the faintest of whispers. And he uttered only one word.

But Rachel heard it.

"Pushed," Milo said. "Pushed."

Rachel sagged against the bed. Milo couldn't know how much that one, simple word meant to her. True, she couldn't do much about it tonight. He was in no shape to talk to the police. But by tomorrow, he might be better. She could take the threatening calendar page to campus security now and tell them that Milo hadn't fallen accidentally. She could tell them he'd been deliberately attacked, and she could tell them that the patient himself could verify that fact.

That had to be enough to get them to listen to her. She had no idea where she would go from there, but it was a start.

Milo opened one eye again, and murmured something.

Rachel didn't catch what he'd said. She leaned down, close to his face. "What did you say, Milo? I couldn't hear you."

"I said," he whispered foggily, "are you Rachel the troublemaker?"

Confused, Rachel decided he was probably on heavy drugs to help him sleep in spite of the pain. She shouldn't be keeping him awake.

But when she moved to leave, he reached out with a bruised arm and weakly grasped her wrist. "Rachel?" he said huskily. And added, with great effort, the words coming slowly, painfully, "After I was pushed, while I was still falling, I heard someone say, 'Perfect. Now I have to deal with that troublemaker, Rachel.' That's what I heard someone say."

Rachel's knees threatened to give. She had to clutch the metal bed rail tightly. "Oh, man," she murmured, shaken to the core by Milo's words.

He took a deep, difficult breath and let it out. "Is that you? Is your name Rachel?"

Her face slate-gray, Rachel nodded silently. "Yes."

"You'd better be careful," Milo whispered. Then his swollen eyes closed.

Rachel stood beside his bed for a few seconds more. "You're right, Milo," she said quietly, gently picking up his arm and slipping it beneath the white sheet. "I'd better be careful."

Chapter 15

Rachel splurged on a taxi ride back to campus. Sitting in the back of the cab, she thought about what Milo had told her.

Why had Milo's attacker said, "And now for that troublemaker Rachel"? She wasn't making any trouble.

The only thing she'd done lately was see images that no one else saw in paintings at the exhibit. And no one had believed that she'd seen them, so how could that make trouble for anyone?

Besides, if the artist didn't want anyone seeing the images, why put them in there in the first place?

That couldn't be it. She hadn't even told anyone that she'd seen something unusual in the still life. Although she *had* stared at it for a long time.

And the only people who even knew she'd

seen the watercolor painting were Aidan and his friends.

Rachel sat up straighter in the back seat of the cab. Her friends . . . Aidan's friends . . . they'd been in the room when she pulled that painting from her purse, and someone, she couldn't remember who, had asked her why she was staring at it for so long.

Still, that didn't mean that the artist who had painted his cruel acts into his art was Aidan or one of his friends, she thought as she leaned her head back against the seat. One of them might have innocently mentioned to someone in the art department that she was seeing things that weren't there in some of the paintings. Might have said, "It's the weirdest thing. We looked and looked, but we didn't see what she saw."

The calendar page had come from the art building. But the art department had many, many students. Any one of them could be determined, for whatever reason, to keep Rachel from living.

If only Milo had seen his attacker's face before he went spiralling down those metal stairs.

The first thing Rachel did when she returned to her room was go to her dresser to retrieve the calendar page. No point in bothering with the watercolor. The police would never see what she saw in that painting. But the painted message on the calendar page was clear enough. That, combined with Milo's testimony when the police talked to him, should convince the authorities that she was in danger.

It wasn't her job to say from whom. It was their job to figure that out. All she had to do was get them to listen to her.

She yanked open the top dresser drawer, where Bibi had said she would put the two items, and reached inside.

They weren't there.

There was only a jumble of socks and headbands and T-shirts and scarves and panty hose and belts.

And although Rachel burrowed deep into the drawer with shaking fingers, tossing items this way and that, there was no sign of the threatening note or the pastel watercolor.

They were gone.

She wouldn't be going to the police for help, after all. Not without any proof.

Shoulders slumped, she slowly closed the drawer. She was turning away from the dresser, disappointment etched across her face, when she heard a sound outside her door. It wasn't the ordinary, everyday sound of footsteps announcing someone's arrival. This sound was softer, almost furtive, the whispering footsteps of someone who preferred *not* to be announced.

The doorknob turned.

Rachel dove into the closet and hid behind the wall of hangered clothes.

She couldn't see, but she could hear. The door opened. Someone came in, very quietly. Walked into the middle of the room. Rachel wanted fiercely to push the clothes aside and peer out, but she was terrified that she'd be seen. Her heart was thudding so loudly in her chest, she wouldn't have been surprised if the intruder had heard it.

She stood in the darkness of the closet, her breath coming in short, panicky little gasps.

What would she do if the stealthy footsteps began approaching the closet? There was no back door, no way out. She would be trapped.

Afraid her erratic breathing was making too much noise in the silent room, Rachel tried to hold her breath. But all that did was make her dizzy.

No footsteps approached her hiding place. After what seemed like hours, she heard movement toward the door. But even after it had opened and closed, Rachel stayed in the closet, afraid it was a trick, afraid he hadn't actually left but was trying to make her think that he had.

It wasn't until her head felt as if she might explode with curiosity that she tentatively pushed the two dresses aside and peered out into the room. It *looked* empty, and she heard no sound beyond her own beathing.

Still, she came out from behind the clothes very slowly, as quietly as possible. And it wasn't until she peeked around the edge of the folding door and saw for herself that the room was completely empty, that she allowed herself a gigantic sigh of relief.

She raced over to the door and locked it.

The telephone rang.

Rachel stared at it as if she expected it to leap off the table and attack her.

It rang again, and a third time.

She answered it.

Aidan's voice said angrily, "I thought you were going to call us to come pick you up at the hospital. I called there, and they said you'd left. You came home by yourself? Why?"

Because right now, I don't know who I can trust, Rachel answered silently. "I caught a cab," she said. "It seemed faster than waiting for someone to drive in from campus. And I know you guys are busy, cleaning up over there."

"Not that busy. I sent Samantha to find you. She there yet?"

If he wasn't "that busy," why hadn't he come himself instead of sending Sam? "No. Haven't seen her."

"I want you to come over here. To the art building. Bibi's here, with Rudy, so I know you're alone. That's not a good idea, Rachel. Wait there for Sam, and then the two of you come back here. You'll be safe here, with us."

So he really did believe that the flowerpot hadn't taken a header off the terrace on its own. It was true, she would be safer at the art building, surrounded by friends.

But she wasn't going to sit around waiting for Sam.

Rachel quickly changed from her dirt-spattered jeans and sweatshirt into clean clothes, and left the room. Instead of taking the elevator, which suddenly seemed a perfect place to become trapped, she decided to take the fire stairs.

No one was in the hall when she pulled the heavy door open, no one behind her when she started down the stairs, her sneakers making little plopping sounds as she descended from one step to the next. The lighting was dim, the stairway cool, the silence comforting because it meant that she was alone. Safely alone.

She had just reached the sixth-floor landing, two floors down, when she heard the first sound. A door opening, somewhere above her. Not far, perhaps two floors up. Someone else had decided against the elevator. Using the stairs for exercise?

Maybe. Rachel continued her descent. The stitches on her anklebone pulled as she stepped down, but the wound itself was still numb from the local anesthetic she'd been given.

Only a second or two later, something struck her about the footsteps above her. They were muffled, much quieter than her own. Like the footsteps that had approached her room. Furtive. Stealthy. Footsteps that didn't want to be heard.

Rachel stopped, lifted her head, looked up. She could see nothing on the landings above her. But when she stopped, the footsteps stopped, too.

Testing, she ran down half a dozen more steps, her ears straining for sound.

The footsteps ran, too.

She stopped again.

They stopped.

No question now. The runner above her knew she was in the stairwell. Had probably seen her from one of the higher landings. Didn't want her to know he was there. And intended to catch up with her.

She had to get off this staircase.

She was on the fifth-floor landing. She whirled, reached out for a doorknob on the heavy metal door, grasped it. It didn't turn. Didn't move.

Locked.

Rachel turned and raced down the stairs to the fourth floor. If the anesthetic injected into her ankle wore off, she was going to be in big trouble. She heard the footsteps racing downward, toward her. Tried the door at the fourth floor.

Locked.

What good was a fire door if it was kept locked?

You can open it from the *inside*, she told herself, in case of fire, but it's locked on the outside for security.

Great.

The footsteps above her increased their speed, uncaring now if they were heard.

Giving up on the door and any hope of leaving the staircase before she reached the ground floor, Rachel increased her own speed, propelling herself down the stairs as if the heat from a roaring inferno was searing her heels.

Chapter 16

By the time Rachel reached the fire door to the lobby, she was drenched in a cold sweat. Her knees were weak from racing down the stairs. And still the footsteps above her persisted, slap, slap, slapping down the stone steps in determined pursuit.

But the lobby door wouldn't be, *couldn't be*, locked. People coming from the basement cafeteria often came up this way and entered the building through this door.

Gasping with relief, Rachel's fingers closed around the metal doorknob.

It turned.

The door opened a crack. And stopped.

Rachel pushed on it, hard.

It wouldn't give.

The door was open only a crack, and although Rachel threw her entire weight against it, it would open no further.

Something was in its way. Something heavy. Something that weighed a lot more than Rachel Seaver.

The footsteps above her had stopped when she did. Gambling that they wouldn't start moving again until she moved, Rachel peered through the opening in the door. Boxes. Stacks of them. She could see tan cardboard boxes, piled high directly in front of the door.

Rachel almost screamed in fury. Who would be stupid enough to bar a fire door?

It wasn't hard to guess what had happened. There had been a delivery to Lester. Supplies of some kind, maybe cleaning supplies or pots and pans for the cafeteria. Whoever had accepted the delivery had carelessly stacked the boxes off to one side, probably not even noticing the fire door was blocked.

The footsteps above her, impatient with the wait, began again on their own. Her pursuer couldn't know the lobby door was barred. He was probably afraid she'd left the staircase, just as she'd intended to. Now he was rushing down to see if his quarry had escaped.

Giving up on the lobby door, Rachel whirled and ran again.

Down still more steps, only one flight this time, to the basement. The only area of the basement she knew well was the cafeteria. Exhaustion and fear had disoriented her and she couldn't remember, as she yanked open the unlocked door and burst into the long, dimly lit hallway, which way she should go. Which way . . . which way? Which way is the cafeteria? she screamed silently, knowing that if she chose incorrectly, she could find herself lost, perhaps trapped, in the basement labyrinth of twisted, turning hallways, boiler and utility rooms, supply and maintenance closets.

There wasn't time to think about it.

Rachel turned to her right and broke into a run. Please let this be the right way, she prayed. Please!

She didn't know whether or not her prayer had been answered until she saw, just ahead of her, another door, this one with a glass window. Could be the door to the outside, could be another locked fire door, in which case she'd be trapped, or it could be the door to the cafeteria, which would mean people and safety.

Although she heard no racing footsteps behind her, she prayed fervently, Please, please let it be the cafeteria. Please don't let it be another locked door. I'm so tired, and my ankle hurts. I can't run anymore. Please make it the cafeteria this time, okay?

She knew her prayer had been answered even before she opened the door, when she glanced hurriedly through the upper glass and saw people sitting at the long, narrow tables eating.

Rachel sagged against the door. She'd made it. She'd be safe in the cafeteria.

Her pursuer must have sensed that, because the sound of footsteps behind her had ended.

Rachel pulled the door open and slipped inside.

She knew she looked like a crazy person — her eyes wide with fear, her breath coming hard and fast, her gait unsteady.

Trying to ignore stares from some of the people she passed, Rachel headed for the main door just as Sam, Paloma, and Joseph entered and looked around the room, their eyes searching. When they saw Rachel, they headed straight for her.

"Where on earth have you been?" Paloma cried as they reached Rachel. "Aidan sent us to get you, and we've been looking all over for you. We were frantic. Sam went to your room, but you weren't there and you hadn't left a note or anything. Rachel, you look terrible!"

Rachel unearthed a tissue from her jeans pocket and swiped at her brow. "You were in my room?" she said to Sam. "When?"

"A few minutes ago. I went in quiet as a mouse because Aidan said you might be sleeping. Rachel, you really should keep your door locked, especially now. I mean, if you really think that someone is after you . . ."

"Did you take the stairs?"

Sam blinked. "What?"

"Did you take the stairs to get down here just now?"

"Rachel, why would any sane person walk down eight flights of stairs when there's an elevator?"

Sam went on about the foolishness of taking stairs instead of the elevator, but Rachel was no longer listening. That had been Sam in her room? Sam, coming in quietly for fear of waking Rachel? Her movements across the carpet hadn't been furtive, after all, but *considerate*?

I hid in the closet from Sam, she thought in disgust. If I hadn't been so paranoid, I could have just walked to the art building with Sam, and never had to go near the fire stairs.

The thought brought tears of frustration to her eyes. How was she supposed to know who to trust? She hadn't learned anything in college so far that had taught her how to behave when she was being terrorized.

They should have a course like that, she thought angrily.

"The calendar page is gone," she told them as they left the cafeteria. "Someone took it.

Bibi put it in the top dresser drawer, and now it's gone. I was going to take it to the police now that Milo can tell them he was attacked, but it's gone."

Paloma stopped in her tracks, her eyes wide. "Milo's conscious?"

Rachel nodded. "So I guess he's going to be okay. He'll tell the police that he was pushed. Just like what I saw in the still life."

"You saw someone being pushed down a fire escape?" Joseph asked.

"Not exactly. It wasn't that clear, not then." She quickly related her nightmare to them. Paloma was horrified, and Sam kept shaking her head. Joseph said nothing.

"It wasn't until I had the dream that I knew Milo had been pushed," Rachel concluded. "Although I think I would have suspected, because by then, I knew that Ted had been attacked on the riverbank."

Rachel felt Sam's eyes on her as they left Lester and headed across campus to the art building. When she turned to look, she saw doubt in them. "You don't believe me?"

"Well, it's just too weird, Rachel. I mean, I'm into all that stuff, you know, dreams and ESP. But I've never heard about anyone like you. Seeing things in paintings that aren't even there? And having dreams about things that haven't happened yet? That's wild."

Paloma was impressed. "You should write a book about it or something, go on talk shows. You could become really famous and make lots of money."

"I'm not a freak, Paloma," Rachel said sharply. "I didn't even know I could do this until now. And frankly, I don't see it as a good thing. It certainly hasn't done *me* any good." It upset her to talk about it. To change the subject, she said casually, "Listen, those smocks you all wear in art, the ones with your names in them? Does anyone have more than one?"

"Oh, those." Sam shrugged. "No, we each only have one, but we don't pay any attention to the names. We just grab the first one at hand. Why?"

"You all wear each other's smocks?"

"Sure. One size fits all." Sam laughed. "Why are you so interested in those ugly old things? They're not a fashion statement, that's for sure."

Rachel digested this bit of information. The paint stains on Aidan's smock meant nothing? Could have been slopped there by anyone in the art department? That seemed like good news.

"Why were you coming in the back door to

the cafeteria?" Joseph asked as they neared the art building. "And how come you looked so terrified? We all thought you'd be sleeping after what happened at the mall. Aidan was really ticked that you didn't call him to come and get you."

Rachel didn't want to tell them about the race down the stairwell. It was too embarrassing, now that she was convinced she'd overreacted. There hadn't been an intruder in her room, after all, only Sam, and probably the person on the stairs really had been out for a little exercise.

"I thought the stairs would be safer than the elevator," she answered, "and then once I got in there, it was so dark and quiet, I guess I got a little shaky and took the stairs too fast."

"Aidan was worried about you," Sam said. "But he couldn't come get you because he was on his way to pick up plaster for his masks. So he sent us instead."

They entered the dim, cool lobby of the art building. All of the work was off the walls, stacked on the floor or lying on tables. Sam glanced around. "Where did Bibi and Rudy go? They were here when we left." She sighed heavily. "We need all the help we can get, wrapping these paintings to take to the mall."

"Well, I can't help," Paloma said. "I have to

go upstairs and finish a necklace I'm working on. I showed Mr. Stein at the jewelry store a sketch, and he loved it. You'll have to get along without me. Want to come with me, Rachel?"

Rachel was about to say, I would rather do almost anything than go upstairs. I haven't forgotten what happened to me the last time I was up there. Just then the elevator pinged and Rudy and Bibi stepped out.

"Oh, great," Paloma said, "you guys can help Sam so I can go upstairs and work." And before anyone could argue, she was in the elevator. Just before the door closed upon her, she called out, "Oh, by the way, good news! Milo Keith is conscious. He's going to be okay. Ask Rachel." Then the sliding doors swallowed her, and the elevator hummed its way upward.

Bibi turned to Rachel. "Rachel, is that true? Is Milo awake? I thought . . ."

"No, he's not," Aidan's voice replied from the entrance before Rachel could answer. "I stopped in to see him on my way back and while I was there, he took a turn for the worse. He's slipped back into his coma. The nurse said they can't be sure he'll come out of it this time."

"Did he say anything to you while you were there?" Bibi asked. "Did he tell you what happened on that fire escape?"

Aidan shook his head. "No. And the nurse

said he hadn't said a word before this relapse."

Wrong, Rachel thought. And realized that Milo's words to her were just one more thing that only she knew about. Her heart sank. She didn't have the calendar page, and now she didn't have Milo's testimony.

She had nothing to take to the police.

Nothing.

Chapter 17

"I'm going to stick this in the dumbwaiter," Aidan said, hefting the fat bag of dry plaster he was carrying, "and haul it on upstairs. How about if we do your mask tonight, Rachel? Now that the exhibit's over, the building will be quiet. I can concentrate better when it's quiet."

Rachel couldn't believe what she was hearing. A mask? He wanted to do a mask? What was wrong with him? Hadn't she insisted she wasn't interested? Especially not with everything that had been going on lately.

"A mask? I don't think so," she said coolly. "Even if I were willing to let someone pour plaster all over my face, which I've already told you I'm not, it wouldn't be tonight, it wouldn't be now, it wouldn't even be anytime soon. I'm still shaking from that flowerpot crashing down on me. I'm far too jumpy to lie perfectly still on a table, Aidan. I'd mess it up for you, so forget it."

He came over to stand beside her. "I know what you're thinking," he said quietly. "That I'm ignoring what's been happening to you. Well, you're wrong. I'm not. But you're safe now, Rachel. You're with friends. I've been itching to do your mask ever since I first saw you, you know that."

Aidan would have argued further, but Samantha interrupted, "Aidan, we've got all of these paintings and masks and sculptures to wrap and pack to take to the mall." She smiled at Rachel. "You can help."

"Sure," Rachel agreed.

Aidan shrugged and moved to the dumb-waiter, pulling on the ropes to haul the bag of plaster up to the tenth floor. Rachel and the others tackled the artwork. Paintings had to be labelled with the artist's name, then wrapped in white plastic and tied with twine. The few works of sculpture had to be handled even more carefully, packed in boxes layered with shredded paper to prevent breakage.

It was a slow process. The light streaming in the windows faded as they worked. They were only half-finished with their task when Rachel glanced over her shoulder toward the front door and was surprised to find the campus completely wrapped in darkness.

"If we don't speed this up a little," Bibi commented as she worked at Rudy's side, "the mall's going to be closed before we get there. Why isn't Paloma helping?"

"She's upstairs working on a necklace," Rachel said.

"Well, I never volunteered to take her place," Bibi complained. "I'm not even an art student. Rudy, go up there and drag her down here."

He was back in five minutes. "Not up there," he said cryptically, and went back to work.

Rachel looked up from the painting she was wrapping. "She has to be up there. We would have seen her if she'd come back down."

Rudy shrugged. "I looked in all the studios. It's dark up there, and quiet. No one home."

No one stopped working, and no one seemed the least bit concerned about Paloma.

"Hey, guys," Rachel said softly, "considering what's been going on, don't you think that when someone isn't where they said they'd be, maybe we should check it out? Why don't we take a break and go find Paloma? Make sure she's okay. I'm not going upstairs alone, so one of you has to come with me."

"You're right," Aidan agreed. "I'll go with you."

His voice was calm, unperturbed, but Rachel's fingers shook as she wrapped slick white plastic around a good-sized painting. None of them had as much reason to be concerned about Paloma as she did. Until they'd seen the note that came with the watercolor, they hadn't believed Ted's death and Milo's fall had been anything but accidental. Even now, Rachel knew they weren't totally convinced the note hadn't been a prank. She could see it in their eyes, hear it in their voices. They were staying with her now because *she* was afraid something bad was going to happen, not because *they* were.

She hurried to finish wrapping the painting. It was one of Joseph's, his favorite, a landscape showing a red barn and a golden hayfield in the distance. She stood it up on end to wrap the white plastic around it. But as she brought the wrap around to the back of the painting where she planned to overlap it, one edge caught on something and stuck.

Rachel sat up straight and looked over the top of the painting for the problem.

There was an envelope, fastened with silver duct tape to the back of the canvas. A white, letter-size envelope.

Any other time, Rachel would have either left the envelope in place and wrapped over it, or she would have called Joseph over to ask if he wanted the envelope removed before the painting went to the mall.

She did neither. Because . . . because this was anything but an ordinary day.

Rachel turned the painting around to face her, using it as a shield from the others, and yanked the envelope free.

Picked at the flap. It wouldn't open. She reached down and picked up the X-Acto knife she'd been using to slice the twine, and slit the flap.

Pulled out two letter-size sheets of white paper, folded in thirds.

She unfolded them.

They were drawings. In charcoal. Sketches, really. Sketches of . . .

Of a figure drowning in a tumultuous sea.

Of another falling down a steep flight of stairs.

In both drawings, the mouth was open in a silent scream, the eyes wide with terror.

There was no background in either sketch. No choppy sea. No stormy sky. No vase. No flowers. Nothing but two separate sketches of two separate tragedies.

Rachel stared down at them. Here, then,

was proof that someone, somewhere, had actually drawn the images she had seen in two oil paintings. Images that no one else had seen. She hadn't imagined them, after all. They were real.

The drawings were dated. Aidan had told her they always dated their work. The dates told quite clearly that the pictures had been drawn prior to the attacks.

Rachel sank back on her heels, the drawings in her lap. What were these sketches doing taped to the back of Joseph's canvas? What did they have to do with him?

She should show the drawings to all of them, to prove that she knew more about art, after all, than they'd thought. But what about Joseph? He must have forgotten where he'd put the sketches. It would be foolish, even crazy, to let him know she'd found them. Rachel lifted her head. Joseph was off to her left, busily wrapping. Samantha was with him, holding a finger over the twine so Joseph could tie a sturdy knot.

He doesn't look like a killer, Rachel thought as she slowly refolded the drawings, slipped them back inside their envelope, and thrust the envelope into the shoulder bag lying at her feet.

But then, Rachel Seaver had never met a killer before and therefore couldn't be a good judge of exactly what one should look like.

She tried to picture Joseph inside that long, black-hooded cape, diving toward Ted on the riverbank, shoving Milo down the fire escape. There was something not quite right about the image.

Rachel couldn't take her eyes off Joseph. The possibility that all this time when she'd believed that she was safe, here in the art building with friends, the killer had been only a few feet away from her, chilled her to the bone.

Joseph? A killer? But he looked . . . he looked so normal!

"We're done!" Samantha said triumphantly, turning away from Joseph. "That's it. Everything is wrapped or boxed." She groaned. "Now all we have to do is load up all this stuff."

"You said we could look for Paloma," Rachel reminded her. She should do something about Joseph. She should make them all aware of the danger in their midst. But how? The first and most important thing was to get Joseph out of the building.

"Oh, sure. Of course. But listen, we don't all need to hunt for her, right?"

"Sure," Rachel said. "Joseph and Rudy can start loading and the rest of us can hunt down Paloma." She had no qualms about leaving

Rudy alone with Joseph. Rudy could take care of himself.

"Good idea," Aidan said, as Joseph and Rudy moved to pick up several wrapped paintings.

"We should split up," Bibi suggested. "Sam and I will take the studios on the ninth floor, Rachel and Aidan the tenth."

Splitting up wasn't at all what Rachel had had in mind. "No, wait!" she hissed, afraid Joseph would hear her. "I need to talk to all of you. When Joseph leaves . . ."

But Bibi and Samantha had already pushed the button to close the doors.

Rachel heard laughing behind her. Thoroughly annoyed with Bibi, she turned around.

Joseph, hefting a handful of paintings, stopped laughing when he saw the look on Rachel's face. "Better get up there," he said, nodding toward the elevator. "Time's running out."

It sounded perfectly innocent.

But Rachel couldn't help wondering if his words held a message, just for her. A reminder that this Sunday was flying by at astonishing, terrifying speed.

And that this Sunday was supposed to be her last.

Chapter 18

The minute the doors closed, Aidan began pressuring Rachel about the mask. "When we find Paloma," he said, one arm wrapped around her shoulders, "we'll send them all off to the mall. We'll have the place to ourselves and we can take our time with the mask. Come on, Rachel, we're not going to have another chance like this again."

Rachel pulled away from him. "I already told you, I'm not going to do it." She reached around to her side for her shoulder bag. When she showed him the sketches Joseph had made, he'd forget all about the mask.

But all her hand found at her side was the edge of her T-shirt. The shoulder bag wasn't there.

Rachel sagged against the wall of the elevator. She knew exactly where the purse was. She had left it lying on the floor. Right where

Joseph could see it . . . pick it up . . . look inside to see whose it was . . . and find the envelope. He would open it, see the sketches, know that Rachel had found them. And that she now knew the identity of the deadly artist.

She had to get to that purse before Joseph did. "Aidan, stop the elevator. *Stop* it!"

Aidan's handsome face reflected his annoyance with her over her refusal to do the mask. "Stop it? This is not a bus, Rachel. You can't just get off anytime you want. I pushed ten, and ten is where the elevator will stop."

"Then press another button!" she shouted. "I have to get off!" Without waiting for Aidan to act, Rachel lunged forward and stabbed the button that said four.

"All right, all right. You don't have to get off. I'll stop bugging you about the mask."

The elevator shuddered to a halt.

Rachel dove for the doors. "It's not the mask. I'll meet you upstairs. I'll explain then."

"Don't you think you're overreacting?" Aidan said.

Rachel knew he was annoyed. She also knew there was no time to explain now. She had to get downstairs. She ran for the stairway door. The thought of another stairwell made her stomach turn over, but waiting for the other elevator would take too long.

It wasn't as if she'd be downstairs alone with Joseph. Rudy would be there. Anyway, she was just going to grab her purse and run for the stairs.

The lobby was empty when she burst out of the stairwell and glanced around hurriedly. Joseph and Rudy were nowhere to be seen.

Rachel raced to the spot where she'd left the purse, prepared to scoop it up, turn and run. She'd go back up to the tenth floor and show Aidan the drawings.

At first, when the purse wasn't where she thought she'd left it, she told herself she'd made a mistake, that she must have moved it and forgotten doing so.

But the shoulder bag, was nowhere to be seen in the lobby.

She *had* to have that purse.

A minute later, she got lucky. Rudy came in to take another load of art to his waiting car outside. To Rachel's relief, Joseph wasn't with him.

Rachel rushed over. "Have you seen my purse?"

"Purse? What purse?"

"Don't tease, Rudy, please. This is important. Didn't you find a big brown shoulder bag on the floor over there? Say you did, please!"

But he shook his dark, curly head. "I didn't find anything."

Rachel sagged in disappointment.

"But Joseph did," Rudy added, deciding not to torment her any further. "He has it."

Joseph had her purse?

"Listen," Rudy said, beginning to move away from Rachel, "I have to go in the back for a minute and get some pads to put on the floor of my trunk before I stick those paintings in there. Joseph will be here in a sec with your purse."

He was going to leave her here in the lobby alone, with Joseph on the way?

Rachel glanced up at the big, round clock high up on one wall. Ten past ten. Less than two hours until Monday. The Monday that she wasn't supposed to "see." It was almost here.

She had lasted this long. And she wasn't stupid enough, after making it this far, to hang around alone in the lobby and wait for Joseph to come in and pick her off like a duck in a shooting gallery. The purse would have to wait. Joseph would, of course, destroy the sketches. Then what would she do for proof?

She saw, in the streetlamp-illuminated darkness outside, a figure approaching the door. Joseph.

She would have to wait until tomorrow to worry about what she'd do for proof now that Joseph had the sketches. Because if she didn't get away that second, there wouldn't *be* a tomorrow for her. YOU WILL NEVER SEE ANOTHER MONDAY.

Rachel turned. Her feet flew across the tile as if they were winged.

She disappeared into the stairwell just as Joseph pushed the big glass door open and strode into the lobby.

So she didn't see Joseph's eyes move toward the stairwell door as it swung shut that last inch or so.

Nor did she see Rudy emerge from the back room just then and follow Joseph's eyes with his own.

Rachel ran up the stairwell until she reached the second-floor landing. Breathless with exertion and anxiety, her ankle throbbing, she knew she could never make it up nine more flights of stairs, and left the stairwell for the elevator. She knew she would be taking a chance. If Joseph had seen her darting into the stairwell, he could already be in one of the elevators, on his way upstairs to find her. The doors could slide open, and there he'd be, standing inside with a wicked smile on his face.

Then he'd grab her and Monday would disappear forever.

Stop it! Rachel commanded. Stop it right now. You can't walk up eight more flights of stairs, and that's that. Joseph won't be on that elevator. He *won't* be.

He wasn't.

No one was. Rachel had the car all to herself, and she stepped into it so awash with relief, she had to grab the railing inside to remain upright.

The elevator would take her to the tenth floor, she'd step out and find Aidan, Bibi, Samantha, and Paloma, tell them what she'd found on the back of Joseph's canvas and, together, they would decide what to do.

If only she had her purse with the drawings inside. Even without the threatening note, even without the watercolor, even without those things, the sketches would have proved one very important thing: that those images, the ones she had described to everyone who hadn't seen them, were *real*.

But she didn't have the purse. Joseph had it.

Still . . . if she could convince Aidan and the others that she was telling the truth, they might help her get that purse away from him before he could destroy the sketches.

He couldn't even say that he had drawn the sketches *after* the fact. Because he'd made the fatal mistake of dating the drawings.

The "ten" button over her head lit up and the elevator slid to a halt.

Feeling more optimistic than she had since the day began, Rachel stepped out of the elevator on the tenth floor.

She turned to the right, toward the studios, and would have hurried down the hall to find Aidan and the others if something very hard hadn't slammed against her skull just then and sent her flying sideways, into the wall.

She made a little sound, half-sigh, high-cry, and slid to the floor softly and quietly, her eyes closing as she fell.

Chapter 19

It took Rachel a few minutes as she gradually stirred back to a dazed consciousness to realize that she was lying down. But not in her own bed. That, she realized instantly. This was much harder and narrower than her own bed.

Was she in the infirmary? She had been hit on the head, she remembered, from behind.

Slowly, very slowly, her awareness increased. And with each new realization, her heart turned colder.

There was something under her neck, something stiff and uncomfortable, poking into the soft skin behind her ears. It felt like cardboard. Cardboard?

Her shoulders ached fiercely.

There was something over her eyes. She had opened them, she was sure of that, but she could see nothing, not even light. The covering felt soft . . . cotton, maybe? Her eyes had been covered with cotton?

And there was, she realized next, something in each of her ears. That, too, felt soft and cottony, and effectively muffled sound, as if she were wearing thick, furry earmuffs. There *were* sounds around her, but she could identify none of them beyond realizing that they weren't infirmary sounds: no ring of a phone at the nurse's desk, no padding rubber-soled footsteps marching across cold, hard tile, no cheerful voice declaring, "Well, aren't *we* looking much better today!"

She was not in the infirmary. The muffled sounds she heard, as if from a distance, were different. The clank of something metal against glass? A spoon, maybe? Footsteps then, but lighter than a nurse's rubber soles. A swishing sound, thick and wet . . . somebody stirring something?

Where *was* she?

Rachel was fully awake now. She moved her neck, trying to ease the discomfort of the sharp, cardboard-y edge poking at her.

"Hold still," a voice said from somewhere above her. "You can't be moving around. You'll ruin everything."

The plugs in her ears, which she was sure were cotton balls, kept her from identifying the voice. She could barely hear it, let alone identify its owner.

What was it that she would ruin if she moved? Maybe she had a broken bone that needed to be set. She had hit that wall pretty hard.

No, if she had a broken bone, she'd be in the infirmary, and she had already decided that she wasn't.

Then why did she have to lie still?

The only way to find that out was to remove the cotton from her ears and the pads from her eyes. Then she would know what was going on.

But when she attempted to lift an arm, she realized why her shoulders ached so fiercely. Her arms were tied behind her back, beneath her. She was lying on her arms. It was not only painful, but it rendered her arms, her hands, completely useless.

She was lying on a table with her arms bound beneath her, her eyes covered, her ears full of cotton. She was completely helpless. The image of herself lying like a trapped animal made her sick in its familiarity.

Because she'd seen that image somewhere before.

The watercolor painting danced before Rachel's eyes, taunting, teasing. You! it seemed to say, you, you, you! It was *you* in the watercolor all along, and you never guessed! And now here you are . . .

Panicking, Rachel began to struggle against the ropes that bound her arms. She bucked and writhed, shaking the table. Her legs were free, so she kicked out with those. She would have tossed her head from side to side, but found that movement impossible with the cardboard collar around her neck.

"Stop that!" the voice above her hissed. "You stop that right now! Maybe you'd better keep in mind that I don't need you conscious to do this. I can do it just as well with you off in dreamland, if that's what you want. I'll be only too happy to send you there myself if you don't lie perfectly still."

Rachel drew in her breath sharply. She knew now, with mind-numbing clarity, what was going on. Didn't want to believe it, had been fighting the thought, but she knew now that continuing to deny it could be disastrous.

It was true. She was the girl in the floral watercolor. She was lying on this table to fulfill the image in that painting, just as Ted had fulfilled the image in the seascape and Milo had done the same for the still life.

Rachel Seaver's face was about to be buried under plaster.

And there was one more unarguable fact, the worst of all. There was nothing in her nostrils. No plastic straws that would enable her to breathe. She could feel the cotton pads over her eyes, which she realized now would be removed the second before the plaster began to pour, when it would no longer matter if she saw her tormentor. And she could feel the cotton in her ears, there so that she wouldn't recognize the voice. Those, too, would be removed before the plaster poured. But she could *not* feel the stiff, sharp plastic of a straw in either nostril.

He wasn't even going to bother with giving her a way to breathe.

Because, as in her nightmare, this was not going to be a *life* mask. This was going to be a *death* mask. And for that, she didn't *need* to breathe.

Rachel lay perfectly still. Because if she was going to have any chance at all of stopping the plaster from being poured over her eyes, her nose, her mouth, her face, she absolutely had to remain conscious. She had to *think*.

Sounds of water running, distant and muted but unmistakable. The clanking of metal against glass, and moist, stirring sounds.

He was mixing the concoction that would soon slop down over her face, hardening quickly, cutting off the last breath Rachel Seaver would ever take.

She wasn't going to see another Monday, after all.

Joseph? Had Joseph seen her slipping into the stairwell? He must have dashed to the other elevator and followed her up.

Except . . . except . . . Rachel struggled to think clearly. Joseph hated making masks. He had said so. It had bothered him, because he hated to admit failure, but he had admitted that he never mixed the plaster correctly, never let it dry the correct amount of time, and once even had to use an X-Acto knife to cut someone's bangs in order to remove a hardened mask.

If Joseph couldn't make a proper mask, would he really choose this way to kill someone?

Anyone could have taped that envelope holding the sketches to Joseph's canvas.

Anyone.

Rachel refused to think about who made the best masks in Salem University's art department. Or about how persistent that great maskmaker had been about creating a mask of her. Or about how annoyed he'd been when she declined.

Her mind focused instead on the X-Acto

knife that Joseph had used to cut someone's bangs.

X-Acto knife.

What had she done with the one she'd used to slit open the envelope?

Rachel's heart beat wildly. *Where* was that knife? Hadn't she slipped it into a back pocket of her jeans?

She groaned silently. It wouldn't do her any good back there.

There had to be some way she could get at that knife. It was her only hope.

Testing, she moved her fingers. If she lifted her lower back the tiniest bit, she could flex the fingers on her right hand.

Could they reach that pocket, the one with the knife inside?

If she stretched them . . .

"Quit moving!" the voice hissed again. "If I have to tell you one more time . . ."

Rachel obeyed. But her heart sank. He must be standing directly over her. How could she wrest the knife from that pocket without moving a hair? She couldn't. Impossible.

There had to be a way to distract him.

The watercolor . . . she focused on that, pictured it in her mind, searching it for details that might be helpful.

And found one.

In her dream, the glass pitcher of mixed plaster had been placed on a smaller table, near the girl's right foot.

Near *her* right foot.

Her right foot was free. No ropes, no straps tying it down.

How could she be sure the pitcher was there? If it wasn't there yet, and she kicked out, he'd realize the folly of placing the pitcher so close to her, and place it somewhere else. What was worse, such a movement would infuriate him and he'd knock her out and continue with the mask.

She heard then, the clanking of metal against glass, and knew he was still mixing. It was so hard to hear clearly with the cotton in her ears. But that sound was sharper than some and she was sure she wasn't mistaken. If she strained with every ounce of her hearing, maybe she could somehow identify the sound of the pitcher being set onto its little table.

Suddenly, he began speaking, stirring the whole time. "You don't understand, I suppose," the voice above her said. "You're not an artist, after all. Most people who aren't won't understand, and a lot of artists won't, either. Narrow little minds never grasp the concept of greatness."

Rachel wanted desperately to fumble for the

knife, but she didn't dare. Instead, she strained to listen over the cottony drone of his voice for the sound of the pitcher being deposited on the little table. Would it be a thud? A clink? What kind of sound should she be listening for?

"The idea came to me late one night when I was alone in the studio. If I could paint things and then make them happen, my art would do more than simply imitate life. It would *be* life. I would be the creator, you see?

"Anyone who can draw a straight line can imitate life. They sit in gardens and paint the flowers as they see them, they paint faces exactly as they are, they paint buildings and bridges and animals and sunsets and seascapes, but they paint them just as they see them. What is creative about that? Nothing. I, on the other hand, paint what I see in my head and then — I create it. My paintings aren't *imitating* life. They're creating it."

No, they're not, Rachel thought, outraged. They're creating *death*. Anyone can do that if they're evil enough.

"You can't imagine, with your tiny little mind," the voice went on, "the power of such an act. So close to the act of creation itself. Of course, I had to be very, very careful. So many tiny minds out there. Wouldn't understand. So

I was careful to disguise the true meaning of the paintings. And, of course, I never signed them. Too dangerous. Actually, Rachel, I never expected anyone to see through them. Certainly not someone as uneducated in art as yourself. You really surprised me."

He was still stirring. "You almost ruined everything. It's a good thing no one listened to you. I love what I'm doing, and I intend to keep doing it. You can't imagine the high I get when I've painted something beautiful and then made it happen. Made it *happen*! What could be more powerful than that?"

"They're not beautiful," Rachel said, unable to stop herself.

The stirring motion halted abruptly, and the voice, when it came, was ominous. Rachel could hear that even through the cotton balls. "What did you say?"

Rachel hesitated. She was taking a terrible chance here. She was lying on this table completely helpless and she was antagonizing him? She was as crazy as he was.

But she had wanted to distract him, hadn't she? Maybe if she made him mad enough, he'd set the pitcher down. "Nobody likes them. That seascape was horrible. Just a lot of blobs of color. Anyone could have painted it, even a six-year-old. I threw it away."

"You *what?*"

"Tossed it in the trash. The incinerator at Lester. Probably already burned to a crisp by now. Exactly what it deserved."

No more stirring sounds. Rage in the voice now. "You stupid girl! I have to have those paintings! I was going to retrieve the seascape when I'd finished with you. You *can't* have destroyed it! I must keep all of them, every single one, as testimonial to the power of my work. Someday, years from now, I will make my power public. To show them. Show them all!" The voice deepened. "You're lying. I can tell you're lying. You never destroyed that painting. You liked it too much. I heard you talking about it."

There it was, finally, the slight, distant thunk she'd been waiting for, the sound of the pitcher being deposited on the table, so close to her right foot.

Rachel didn't waste a second. Keeping the image in the watercolor in her mind, she threw her right foot sideways to where she thought the pitcher should be.

Her aim was accurate. She felt the pitcher as her foot slammed into it, heard the splashing sound as the pitcher went flying, imagined the plaster spraying in a white, milky arc out across the room, heard the shattering sound as the pitcher smashed into the hard, unyielding tile and exploded into a million pieces.

Heard him scream, wild with rage.

Rachel wondered how many more seconds she had to live.

Chapter 20

He screamed, he shouted, he shook the table.

But he didn't kill her.

She knew why. If he killed her now, without the mask, the image in the watercolor would mean nothing. There'd be no "high," no heady rush of power, no swollen ego.

Furious as he was, he was willing to wait for what he wanted, needed, had to have.

And the sink was on the far side of the room, under the wide, low windows. He had to go over there to get more water if he was going to mix up a new batch of plaster.

Plaster . . . Rachel remembered Aidan tugging on the dumbwaiter ropes, hauling a brand-new bag of plaster upward.

She pushed the image from her mind.

All senses alert now, Rachel could hear faint mopping and wiping sounds as he cleaned up the mess on the floor. As long as the sound continued, she knew he was working on the tile, his back to her as he knelt below her table.

Free to move now, she wriggled her fingers this way and that, stretching them as far as she could in hopes of reaching the jeans pocket and the X-Acto knife. There wasn't much time. Soon enough, he'd stand up and see her wiggling about, know she was up to something. He'd find the knife and take it from her, and she would have no hope then. None.

Desperate, she lifted her back a fraction of an inch higher to give her hands more room, and suddenly, there it was, the edge of her pocket.

There was no time to be careful. She slid the knife out, and then carefully pressed the button to release the blade.

"I don't have much time. People are going to be looking for you," the voice said, and Rachel could tell that he was standing up now, then moving to the sink, probably dripping a trail of wet plaster every step of the way.

How thick were the ropes that bound her? Rachel wondered.

Not very, as it turned out. He had simply wound a single strand of twine around her wrists. It took her no more than a few seconds to slice through it with the knife.

Her hands were free.

But he mustn't know that. She wanted more than anything to reach up and pull the cotton from her eyes, to see him clearly, to know who this monster was, this maniac who killed for the sheer power of it. All in the name of art.

But a look wasn't worth giving away her newfound freedom. She needed to catch him by surprise.

Rachel could barely control her trembling as she waited, waited, the knife firmly gripped in her fingers. She heard water running, heard the familiar clink of metal on glass. He'd gotten another pitcher, poured fresh plaster into it, added water at the sink, and was stirring angrily, furiously.

He'd be in a hurry now to fulfill his mission. She had, for just that one second when she'd kicked out at the pitcher, taken away his power. How he must have hated that! He must need more than ever to create the image in the watercolor, to get that feeling of power and control again.

She would have to be fast, so fast . . .

If only she could remove the pads from her eyes.

But not yet . . . not yet . . . he mustn't know her hands were free.

Her ears ached with the strain of such intense listening. Just a few more minutes . . .

Footsteps . . . approaching her table . . . the sloshing of the mixed plaster . . .

"Now, you lie perfectly still," he said, his voice icy, "or I'm going to kill you right here and now and do your mask afterward."

She waited just a fraction of a second and then brought her hand out from behind her and slashed out blindly with the razor-sharp X-Acto knife.

A scream of pain and rage told her she'd connected.

Still holding the knife, Rachel threw herself sideways, off the table and onto the floor. As she fell, the pads over her eyes slid sideways and then, as she jumped to her feet, dropped to the floor.

She could see.

And the person standing before her, staring in disbelief at the gashed, bleeding arm held up, dripping red on the tile floor, wasn't Aidan McKay, not Joseph Milano, not even Rudy Samms.

It was Samantha Widdoes.

They stared at each other, Rachel's eyes stunned, Samantha's hot with rage.

"You?" Rachel managed. "*You*? I don't understand. Why?"

Samantha grabbed a smock from the table behind her and wrapped it around her wounded arm. Her mouth twisted as she sneered, "You don't know what it was like! No one appreciated my work! They all said it was weak. 'Wishy-washy pastels,' Joseph called them. But I can't work in oils. You heard them at the exhibit. Everyone hated that seascape. They all said my paintings were weak."

"Sam . . ."

"Well, I showed them, didn't I?" Samantha's perfect cheekbones were an angry scarlet. "Weak? *Weak?* When I can paint something and then make it happen! *They* can't do that, none of them. I'm the only one who can. I'm the one with all the power."

Rachel's mind raced. She had to get out of this room. But Sam was standing between her and the door. And she was so full of rage and hate, that even with a wounded arm, Rachel would be no match for her. "But Sam," she said softly, "no one *knows* you've got that power, so what good does it do you? You didn't sign the paintings, and I was the only one who saw the hidden images. You should tell everyone. You should share your power, so they'll know."

A crafty smile lit Samantha's face. "Oh, no. I thought that, too, at first. But that would spoil everything. I'd have to stop then, and I don't want to. Not for a long, long time. It's enough for me that *I* know. That's why I have to kill you, Rachel, because you saw the images. I thought I hid them so cleverly." She tilted her head at Rachel, the expression on her face one of simple curiosity. "Why was it only you who saw them? You don't know anything about art."

"Maybe that's why." Rachel reached out slowly, easily, to place both hands on the edge of the table. She knew it was on wheels, because it had moved slightly beneath her when she was trying to wrestle the knife from her pocket. "I wasn't judging your work artistically, like the others were. I was just looking at the painting to see what was in it."

"And you found it," Sam said, a trace of regret in her voice. "Well, that's too bad, Rachel. I like you. I think we could have been friends. But I have no choice now. You can see that, can't you?" Her voice hardened, "I'm *not* giving up my power."

"But . . ." Rachel said, desperately trying to stall for time. "How did you start your . . . creating?"

"It was an accident in the beginning," Samantha said.

Rachel's grip on the table tightened.

"I had this vision of someone standing on the riverbank fishing, of someone pushing him over the edge toward the waterfall, and so I sketched it. The drawing was so much more exciting than stupid, pale flowers. Joseph would have loved it."

Rachel apologized silently to Joseph. The sketches hadn't been his, but Samantha's.

"Then I painted the image into the seascape, so cleverly that no one would notice. And later I took the baseball bat and went looking for someone fishing. I knew there'd be someone there, and I didn't care who it was. I didn't even know Ted Leonides. When I'd done what the vision told me to do, I felt so strong, so powerful, Rachel. It was wonderful! And," Samantha shrugged, "I knew I'd get another vision. And I did." She laughed, a thin shrill sound. "That's why Milo's in the hospital." She looked at Rachel again, her eyes bright. "You knew Milo had been pushed, didn't you? How did you know he hadn't just fallen?"

"It's a gift," Rachel said flatly, unwilling to share "visions" with this cold-blooded, power-hungry maniac.

"They said my work was weak," Samantha said almost absentmindedly, as if she were talking to herself. "Weak! Which meant that *I* was." To Rachel, she said slyly, "But I'm not, am I, Rachel? You'd testify to that if you could, wouldn't you?"

"No," Rachel said calmly. "I'd testify that

you are a weak, sneaky little coward."

Samatha's cheeks flamed, and her eyes turned dark with fury. "Get back on the table," she commanded in a completely different voice, this one hard and cold. She seemed unaware that Rachel's hands had a firm grip on the table's edge. "You're not going to ruin this for me."

"Yes," Rachel said, "I am." And with one strong, desperate push, she shoved the table forward, pinning a startled Samantha between it and the smaller table behind her.

With a roar of rage, Sam lunged forward to push herself free. But the floor beneath her was still wet and slippery from the spilled liquid plaster. She slipped, slid, her feet went out from under her, and with a look of total surprise on her face, she slammed to the floor. There was a sudden, sickening crack as the back of her skull hit the hard tile. Then silence.

Shaking violently, Rachel stayed where she was for several seconds, expecting Samantha at any second to jump to her feet and attack.

But nothing happened.

Slowly, tentatively, Rachel moved around the edge of the table to look down.

Samantha lay on the floor, her eyes closed. Her face was free of rage now, and seemed peaceful and sweet. Innocent. Even . . . even gentle. The real Samantha, the cruel, power-mad Samantha, was hiding now, like the images in her gentle, innocent watercolors.

But she had been unmasked. And no amount of plaster in the world could hide who she really was.

Rachel glanced up at the big, round clock high on the wall.

Twelve-ten.

Monday.

It was Monday.

And she was alive.

Rachel stepped around Samantha and left the room.

Epilogue

They stood in the art building lobby, watching as Samantha was taken away on a stretcher. Aidan had an arm around Rachel, who was pale but steady on her feet, and Rudy and Bibi, visibly shaken, were holding hands.

"She picked Milo almost at random," Rachel said. "The night of the party, she must have scouted the house, checked out the rooms and picked his because it was right on the fire escape. So she could fulfill the image she'd hidden in the watercolor."

Rachel knew that none of her friends were grasping what had happened. They had known Samantha longer than they had known Rachel, and had had no inkling of Samantha's hidden rage about her work. They were all in shock.

There would be plenty of time later to fill them in, explain that Sam had locked her in the closet, left the charm on her pillow, pushed the heavy pot off the terrace, sent the calendar page, tried to kill her because Rachel alone saw the hidden images in the paintings.

They would believe it now. They wouldn't understand about her dreams and her ability to see in Samantha's paintings what no one else had, but that didn't matter. Not really.

She was certain of one thing. Now that she had stopped the fulfillment of the worst nightmare of all — her own murder — she would have no more dreams. She felt it in her head and in her heart. They were finished.

The lobby should have seemed barren and cold, with all of the paintings off the walls in preparation for a new exhibit. But to Rachel, it seemed, for the first time since she'd seen the seascape hanging on the far wall, warm and welcoming.

She would come back here again.

She might even come back in the morning.

Monday seemed like a good day to begin learning about art.

About the Author

"Writing tales of horror makes it hard to convince people that I'm a nice, gentle person," says **Diane Hoh**.

"So what's a nice woman like me doing scaring people?

"Discovering the fearful side of life: what makes the heart pound, the adrenaline flow, the breath catch in the throat. And hoping always that the reader is having a frightfully good time, too."

Diane Hoh grew up in Warren, Pennsylvania. Since then, she has lived in New York, Colorado, and North Carolina, before settling in Austin, Texas. "Reading and writing take up most of my life," says Hoh, "along with family, music, and gardening." Her other horror novels include *Funhouse*, *The Accident*, *The Invitation*, *The Fever*, and *The Train*.

Return to Nightmare Hall . . .
if you dare

Student Body

We were all so very sorry.

If only we could have changed what happened. In a second, in a minute, in a heartbeat, we'd go back to that blustery night in late March and correct our horrible mistake. Then everything would be the way it was before.

Before the fire.

Because afterward, nothing would ever be the same again.

All it takes is one careless accident that sets the wheels in motion. In one fleeting moment everything is changed. Forever. And you don't even know it's happening. You're laughing and talking and goofing around, and you don't even realize until it's too late.

When you *do* see what's happened, you wish and you hope and you pray to go back, just for that one moment, to do something differently, to erase the horror that came after. You actually kid yourself that it might be possible. But, of course, it isn't.

We thought we could learn to live with our mistake.

How could we know that someone didn't want us living with it?

How could we know that someone didn't want us *living* at all?

Being sorry wasn't enough.

Someone wanted more, much more.

Someone wanted us *dead*.

NIGHTMARE HALL

where college is a scream!